SURRENDERED IV

BY

PEGGY PATRICK

ISBN-10: 996295933
ISBN-13: 978-0-9962959-3-2

Cover Design by Charlene Raddon
Http://cover-ops.blogspot.com

This one is for Cody...my son, who I am extremely proud of. His fun-loving sense of humor was my inspiration for the hero in this novel.

SURRENDERED IV

CHAPTER ONE

Donny Thorn Brandon reached across the seat of his well-used, but good, crew cab Ford dually and ran his hand gently down his wife's thick blonde hair. He had to lean over to reach her. He wished he could think of something to say that would reassure her, but he was about as blank as he'd ever been. A little reassurance aimed *his* way about now wouldn't hurt his feelings any.

Jesse had always been good for that. In fact, his older brother had mostly raised him, after their mom died when he was twelve and had sent him off to college a few weeks ago. *Or was it months.* Except that he never made it to college.

Known all of his life around home at High Point Dude Ranch as Donny, he was use to having his direction switched suddenly. But this! He glanced at Reeny Carr, now Reeny Brandon, where she sat curled against the truck door. This had caught him completely by surprise. He just prayed that his brother would still have the same loving attitude when he arrived back home fifty miles from now, as he had when he left out for Phoenix, Arizona a couple of weeks ago. He always got an eye-roll from Jesse over his quick-change plans...not quite grasping his younger brother's relationship with his God.

His first encounter with his Heavenly Father came as a young boy. It happened the day of his mother's funeral, after a short lifetime of being attached at the hip to his mom. His and Jesse's dad had deserted the family years before. Donny had lain on top of the fresh mound of dirt and flower wreaths and refused to leave the cemetery. He had cried off and on for hours, hugging the new grave, until sometime in the wee hours of the next morning, he heard a strong, but comforting voice whisper in his ear. *"**Go with Jesse**."* He had stopped crying and raised his head to look around in the early morning darkness. No one was there. He stood up and in the moonlight recognized his big brother squatted down about fifty yards away on the far side of the small cemetery, watching and waiting. Jesse stood up and Donny ran into his arms.

Jesse was about eight years older than Donny and became more like a dad than big brother, raising him on hard work and good manners on his struggling dude ranch in Wyoming.

He hadn't forgotten for a minute, the voice he'd heard that night at his mother's gravesite. He knew somehow that it was the Almighty that had spoken to him and he wanted to know more about Him. He'd heard that Voice many times throughout his teen years, but learned to keep that part of his life private. As so many other times, it was that Voice, sometimes in the form of an inner compelling, that caused him to switch directions mid-stream. It had always been small changes now and again, and with no hesitation on his part, he obeyed. If he believed God said it, he did it.

But *this* time was not small.

He watched his young troubled wife, who wasn't much younger than he was, sleeping, her slight body curled tightly in a wad as though trying to hide from view. Only God knew how he was going to handle this situation. Only God.

A long slow sigh escaped from deep down and he turned to the customary scenery whizzing past his window for comfort. Home. He'd only been gone a month, but it looked like even the landscape had changed its face. He could have been a stranger cruising this highway of his young teen years for all the familiar comfort it afforded him now. He knew nothing was physically different out his window, but everything seemed different. Maybe it was him. Of course it was him! What he'd discovered since he'd first laid eyes on Reeny Carr had been enough to well age him overnight. He felt like he'd lived much longer than his twenty-two years. Not only had he left his youth a ways behind him, but he was going home with a new name—and family, to boot!

Jesse had long planned for his little brother's college education. That was going to happen if the whole ranch fell in and Donny never argued the point, even though he was never fully satisfied that off at college was where he belonged. He had searched for the best school for his intended studies in Theology. He'd known for most of his young life that God had called him to preach and Grand Canyon University in Phoenix, Arizona seemed to be calling his name.

He had been in Phoenix less than one day when his plan was abruptly changed. Right in the middle of a huge bite of cheeseburger in the heart of the city, he nearly sucked it all down his windpipe when that gentle voice deep inside rose up… **Go to Albuquerque**.

"Now!?" He sputtered bits of his burger onto the dash of his truck.

It wasn't that he wasn't fairly well prepared for these out-of-the-blue modifications, but geez-louise, he only had a couple of days to get registered at the University. Then he remembered that Grand Canyon University had an Albuquerque location. He swallowed the disappointment down with the rest of his lunch and got out his map. Another full day's drive ahead of him.

A heavy sigh escaped as he pulled back onto the road and said aloud, "Lead on, Lord." Under his breath, he muttered, *I've got to be nuts.*

It wasn't until a full week later while sitting in a Hampton Inn on the outskirts of Albuquerque where the Lord had instructed him to go and WAIT, did he finally decide he *was* nuts. He suddenly couldn't wait another second. He had to get out of there. Obviously he'd been run around in circles by stupid voices in his head and missed college registration which he now had no desire for anyway. He was going home!

He stopped in the motel dining room for a late breakfast before leaving. And true to form, just as he stuck a monster spoonful of oatmeal in his mouth, he heard the unmistakable Voice of his Heavenly Father say, **Paradise**.

Paradise? What does that mean? And why does He always talk when my mouth is loaded?

He finished eating and swallowed the last of his luke warm coffee, and headed out. Then it came again.

Paradise.

Sometimes he wished he wasn't so sensitive to hearing the Voice of the Lord. It was, on one hand, his greatest source of joy and excitement. But the other hand was just the opposite. It had cost him dearly as this closeness developed between him and God. Cost him his young friends through the years and the endurance of blank stares and head shakings from others. No one could relate to this relationship he had. And didn't want to. Except for Judd Luke. The cowboy preacher who lived on a neighboring ranch had had a few serious encounters with God and seemed to genuinely understand where Donny Brandon was coming from.

Too late he realized he'd missed his turn. Great. All he wanted right now was to go home, almost to desperation. Maybe that was it! High Point Dude Ranch was like a paradise to him. His big paint mare between his legs was like Heaven. Riding and roping and branding, mainly for the Lukes on the Double OO, was his hearts passion. And the dudes that came for a few days of playing cowboys and cowgirls was pure fun. Always good for a lot of laughs.

About the same moment that he'd decided that was God's way of telling him to go home, he noticed that he was driving down...*Paradise Boulevard?* And on the wrong side of Albuquerque to where he should be to go home. His heart rate kicked up a few notches as he sensed something strange was happening. Just had no clue what.

Okay cowboy, relax and breathe. Keep driving.

Shortly, his eye went to a small sign that read *Paradise Park.* Without thinking about it, he pulled through the entrance and pulled up beside a picnic table and parked. The place appeared deserted. Eerily quiet. It wasn't a big place. There were lots of large trees dotted throughout maybe four or five acres, other picnic tables, a sand pit for volleyball and some type of small community center building on the other side of the park from where he was.

He got out and leaned against his left front fender, arms crossed over his chest, one booted foot resting over the other one. *Now what?* He pushed his black Stetson up and back to afford him a fuller view of his surroundings. Not much here.

The sound of an approaching vehicle made him turn half around to check it out. It was a late model black Lincoln Continental with dark tinted windows that concealed the interior. It slowed almost to a stop behind his dually before squealing its tires on acceleration. He watched until the car disappeared behind the building across the park. Probably a public restroom back there, he decided, and dismissed the whole thing.

Seconds later, just as he was beginning to feel ridiculous, a young girl with long blonde tangled hair, dressed in very short tan shorts and a white, dirt smudged fitted t-shirt stepped from behind the base of a large tree about 20 yards from his truck. She looked around frantically before running straight for the dually. Without so much as a glance at Donny, she jerked open the passenger back door and dove inside pulling the door closed behind her.

He stood frozen, staring into the windshield, but couldn't see any movement inside the vehicle.

Drive away Thorn.

He felt like a big fist just landed in his gut. *Thorn?* He turned a complete circle in the same footprints where he stood. *Thorn?* Where did that name come from? He knew *where*. But *why?*

He got in the truck and backed out and drove back onto the main street without creating any undue attention. He would not know the girl was back there if he hadn't seen her get in. She made no sound whatsoever.

Lord, what's going on here?

0An image of the black Lincoln popped into his mind. Was she running from whoever was in that car? He drove on until he felt safe enough that whoever she was hiding from was left behind.

Thinking she might be hungry, he pulled to the drive-thru of the next burger joint he came to. Without looking behind him, he said, "What would you like to eat, young lady?" She didn't answer nor move from her hideout in the back floor board.

He tried again. "I'm buying. Come on…tell me what you like to eat."

Not a sound.

"Mam, unless I'm about to be red-faced all the way to my ankles, it looked to me like you've got more than one mouth to feed back there." In fact, there was no mistaking her baby bump beneath that clinging t-shirt. Still no answer.

He pulled to the window and ordered burgers, fries and milk shakes for both of them. Five minutes later he parked in the middle of a crowded supermarket parking lot to blend into the mass of vehicles until he could figure out what to do with his pretty little pregnant passenger. And eat!

"Okay. You can come out now. Lunch is served." He laid everything out on the console, stuck straws into the lids on the shakes, then craned his neck around and looked over the seat back. What he saw made his heart jerk hard.

The girl looked like a little child curled into a ball in the floor. Her head rested on the hump in the middle, her blonde hair disheveled with leaves and twigs poking in the tangles. But it was the way her arms were cradling around her stomach, protecting and comforting her unborn baby that grabbed his heart. Her steady even breathing told him she was sound asleep.

There was no telling how long it had been since she'd slept or had anything to eat. Or had a bath. She was definitely on the run and God sent him to help her out. That was all he knew for sure.

With lunch packed back up, he headed down Highway 25 with not a clue one where to go. He couldn't just haul this girl to Wyoming. She possibly lived here. And right now, she couldn't help him out any. Until he could figure this out, he decided he'd better stay in town.

A few minutes later he parked in the only space left for motel guests and went around to help her get out. At least she could sleep in a decent bed and get some food in her. Then he'd find out where she belonged.

He patted her shoulder to awaken her, not prepared for her reaction of instant fight mode. Both feet shot out, landing a bruising blow to both of his upper legs.

Ahh…that was too close!

She raised up and at the same time her fists each popped a one-two punch right in his nose and chin, then she slid out of the truck floor and started to run. Donny was quicker and caught her in the crook of his arm.

"Hold on a minute. You're safe. It's ok."

She struggled against his hold.

"You're safe. Nobody's going to hurt you."

She relaxed and after a few seconds, he let his arm fall to his side.

"I'm Thorn Brandon." *Did he just introduce himself as Thorn? What the…*

"I…I'm Reeny…Carr. I'm sorry about this. I'm…I'm just so tired. I'm sorry…I"

The girl was obviously sleep deprived. "Look, I've got you a room here. And something to eat. Why don't you go in and shower and get some good sleep. You can lock yourself in."

She glanced back inside the truck, then up at Donny. She smelled the burgers.

He grinned and nodded. "How about let's eat first."

She hadn't eaten in two days. Or slept either. She raked her hair back from her face and came away with leaves between her fingers. "Oh..." The realization of how dirty and tired she was suddenly overwhelmed her and tears rolled muddy streaks down her face.

Donny's arm automatically came up around her shoulders. "Come on. You'll feel better after you get some food in you."

They both settled up front and Reeny devoured her's and half of his before a sudden urge to be sick waved through her.

Donny got her to her room seconds before she hurried into the bathroom and threw up. When she came out, he was still standing there, hat in hand.

The room had double King beds and Reeny feebly curled up on the one close to the door. "You can have the other bed," she stated. "I need close to the bathroom."

Before he could think what to do next, she was asleep.

He continued to stand there and stare at her while he twisted his hat round and round in his hands. The biggest part of her was her pregnant belly. And that thick, tangled mop of buttery looking blonde that was on her head and splayed all over her pillow was running a close second. He would step over there and pull a few twigs out of it just to feel it, but his bruised left nostril was screaming...*don't do it!*

Donny had always been about fun and games. If there was a laugh or a joke in it, he was usually the instigator. But this wasn't funny. He wasn't even trying to find the humor in Reeny Carr. Maybe for the first time in his life, he did not want to lighten up a hurting heart with laughter. Not today. He had wanted, almost overwhelmingly so, to pull those muddy tears into his arms and dry them on his t-shirt front. But he restrained himself in fear of scaring her. She was already scared and he was a stranger. He didn't want to leave this room. Didn't want to let her out of his sight.

He raised his hands and hat in a gesture of helplessness and looked upward. Then he stepped over to sit on the edge of *his* bed and wait.

This is Your deal here, Lord. I have no clue what You want me to do. I need to make sure she's safe. How am I supposed to help her? To protect her and her baby? How?

Marry her.

For a long, desperate minute, he stared into the space of the room before he realized he wasn't breathing. Then he decided his mind was trying to make this into a joke. He shook his head and tried to clear his thoughts. Suddenly the question of his name came to mind.

Lord, what's up with calling me Thorn?

He had been called by his first name only his entire life. Even though his birth certificate had his full name, Donny Thorn Brandon—Thorn was never to be used or mentioned, especially around Jesse. Their dad had named him that with a derogatory meaning behind it. He never wanted either of the boys and left them for their mom to raise alone right after Donny's birth. But not before he named the last little *thorn* in his side. Jesse had been old enough to understand the meaning behind the name and wouldn't allow him to use it except on legal paperwork. Now he wondered if his own mind was playing a practical joke on him. That wasn't God saying, Marry Her. That was just nuts! So. He probably never called him Thorn either.

So with that reasoned out, he used a little more practical thinking and locked Reeny in the room and walked across the street to Walgreens and picked up a few necessities for her, like toothpaste, toothbrush, hair brush, plus a few more items. A rack of loose flowing, knee length silky dresses caught his eye and he grabbed the smallest size they had and stuffed everything in a pink shopping bag. A basket of little fuzzy teddy bears sat beside the checkout. He selected a pink one and a blue one and dropped them in Reeny's bag. That should cover the baby, either way.

A couple minutes later he set the bag on the lamp table between the beds. Reeny hadn't moved a muscle since she'd laid down. He couldn't help but notice how pretty she was. The structure of her body was cute. Attractive. Small boned and vulnerable to anyone who might want to hurt her. Only God knew who would want to do that, but he wasn't born last week. The world was full of bullies. Evil bullies.

He pulled the bed spread up from the bottom of the bed and covered her, then pulled off his boots and stretched out on the opposite bed. He'd already made up his mind to stay in the same room. God Himself would have to tell him to leave, three times, before he could bring himself to leave her there.

Reeny opened her eyes and blinked several times into the blackness of some room where she was under covers on a bed. Where was she? She sat up, but couldn't see. *Oh God! Oh God!* She frantically felt of her seven months protruding stomach, then jumped up in full panic mode. Something akin to a sob tore from her throat just as a light popped on behind her.

"Reeny?"

The deep male voice coming from the room threw her legs into high gear and she raced for the open door a few steps in front of her and slammed it shut behind her.

Donny saw the bathroom light come on under the door and heard the lock click. He knocked softly on the door. "Reeny?" He could hear a muffled crying, like she had her face in a towel. The sound was close to hysteria. "Reeny?"

More suppressed moaning.

"Reeny, it's Thorn Brandon." *Thorn.* He did it again, and then remembered that was the name she knew him by. "You're safe, honey. You're in a motel room, remember? You hitched a ride in the back floor of my truck. I brought you here so you could rest." She wasn't making a sound now. "Reeny?"

To his astonishment, the door swung open and a sheer panic stricken, tear stained face looked up at him, then the girl threw herself in his arms and held on for dear life. He held her against him, letting the safety of his tight bear hug work its calming medicine. She sobbed into his chest, wetting his t-shirt. Only after the crying stopped did he release her enough to look down at her. She was beautiful, even all smudge-faced.

He glanced at the lighted dial on his watch just before he cupped her face in his hands and brushed at the lingering tears with his thumbs. "I don't know who you're running from, Reeny Carr, but I'm here to protect you and help you. Nobody is going to hurt you."

She exhaled slowly. "I'm not afraid of you. I…just…thank you for helping me."

"You're welcome. Do you want to talk? Tell me what's going on?"

She was thoughtful for a moment, then slowly nodded. "Yes, but I'm so tired. It's not daylight yet."

"No, it's just after midnight. Long time before daylight."

"I think I'll take a shower now."

"Alright." He reluctantly turned loose of her and stepped back. "Oh, by the way, I picked up a few things for you." He got the pink bag and handled it to her. If you need something else, let me know."

She took the bag from him, never taking her eyes from his. *Was this cowboy for real? Maybe he's an angel. Not really human.* "Thank you," she said and headed for the shower.

Behind the locked bathroom door, Reeny's hands shook as she took out each item from the bag and set them on the vanity. She held the dress against the front of her and stared at the image in the mirror. She had similar dresses and silky wraps and such. Things she never wanted to see again. But this little dress made her feel different inside. Clean. Pretty. She draped it over the towel rack, reached into the bag and came out with a single pair of nylon panties on a hanger. She smiled, surprised at that find. When she pulled out the teddy bears, she melted in disbelief. One hand automatically cupped around her belly. *Oh, my. He bought my baby a gift.* Seeing the pink and blue made her realize that she'd never given thought to what sex her baby was. Hiding the fact that she was pregnant had been priority until a week ago. Then when it was discovered, she worried about how to keep her baby from being taken away.

Until this moment, she hadn't been able to fully consider that she was about to become a mother. She would soon have a son or a daughter. What she *did* know was that she loved this tiny baby more than her own life. It had been the single most important thing in her existence since the day she knew for sure it was inside of her.

For so long she'd fought for her baby's life. To get away from a man who would want her baby dead or gone. Then suddenly she is in the company of a strange man who bought her unborn child a teddy bear. The only reason she could trust this man at all was because he didn't stop and pick her up. She sort of picked him up. And strangely she felt safe with him. She had no idea this type of man existed. He hadn't even tried to touch her body.

Forty minutes later, Reeny came out wearing the dress, her long blonde natural curls clean, towel dried and cascading down her back.

Donny thought he had never actually seen a truly beautiful woman before this moment. Her lashes were long and light, her skin pink with a fresh scrubbed glow. The little black and white flowery dress fit her like it should. Perfect.

He wanted to know her story. Where did she come from? Where was her family? Who was she hiding from? Her pain and fear was so obviously raw. But he was here for her now, whatever that panned out to mean.

"Thank you, Thorn, for everything. That was so thoughtful...to buy something for the baby." She held up both bears where she held them in one hand.

"You're welcome, Reeny. You look nice in that dress. I'm glad it fit."

She smiled slightly and then slid between the sheets of her bed. A lump formed in her throat at the compliment Thorn gave her. She cuddled both bears against her chest and was soon asleep.

He switched off the lights and followed suit, more exhausted than he realized.

Reeny felt her heart hammering her awake. She couldn't see in the darkness, but it was clear that someone was inserting a card key into the door lock. The door handle was rattling like someone was twisting it back and forth. She froze in fear, unable to even call out for Thorn. But she didn't have to. She heard him get up and head for the door about the time a female voice was heard giggling and obviously intoxicated.

"That's not our room, you idiot."

More giggling was heard and finally the partiers moved on.

Reeny hadn't moved and Donny assumed she had slept through it. He went back to bed.

It took everything she had to suck a good breath and make her arms and legs move. She hated this choking fear, but she'd lived with it for a long time. Only the past few months it had become paralyzing.

Finally she forced herself to sit up, and then hurried around the end of her bed to Thorn's. Not asleep yet, he heard her before he saw her form beside his bed.

"Thorn?" she whispered.

The consuming fear he heard in her voice broke his heart. He held up the spread he was under and she slid in. His arm went around her middle, just above her extended belly and scooted himself closer until she was spooned into the curve of his body. She was trembling and he held her tightly until she finally slept.

***

CHAPTER TWO

Donny woke to thunder and lightning and a torrential downpour. And no bed partner. The bathroom light was off. Reeny's bed was empty. He glanced at his watch as his feet hit the floor. Seven A.M. He glanced at the television stand where he'd left his personal stuff. The truck keys were there beside his wallet. But the room key was gone.

He pulled on his boots while he hop skipped to the door. By the time he jerked it open and ran out into the hallway, Reeny rounded the corner carrying a cardboard tray with two coffees and cinnamon rolls.

The sight of Thorn in panic mode stopped her in her tracks. "Is...is something wrong?"

He couldn't speak or move for several seconds. He was trying to get a grip on the craziness rushing his heartbeat. He'd barely met this girl, but it didn't feel that way. He felt a connection to her that didn't make sense. Was there really such a thing as love at first sight? That's what this seemed like. Like

Reeny belonged with him. And the baby. The baby, too. His heart swelled to bursting at the thought.

"Thorn?" Reeny stood still holding the tray and waited for him to say something. He looked like a wild man with a head full of black hair sticking out everywhere, sleep still plastered to his facial features and looking like he could attack a grizzly and win.

"I just wondered where you went." He tried to sound casual as he took the tray from her.

"Well, it was my turn to buy." Reeny grinned at him as she led the way back into the room.

"Oh, well, thank you, mam." He knew the motel offered a *free* breakfast. He was glad to see her feeling better. Catching up on her rest seemed to have brought out some sassy. He liked that.

Sitting on the sides of their beds each facing the other, they dug in. She glanced up from her giant cinnamon roll to see Thorn finished and watching her eat.

"Good morning." His voice was early morning gravelly.

She managed a slight smile with her mouth full. "Mo-ning," she muffled out.

A lopsided grin slanted across his mouth. Was there anything unattractive about this woman? Why did his heart swell so tight at the least little thing she did, like mutter with her mouth full.

Suddenly the thought hit him that she might be running from an abusive husband. He needed a reality check and right now. He didn't know one simple thing about her except the obvious. Number one, she's running scared and number two, she's very pregnant. Then very quietly, he was reminded of a third fact. **Drive away Thorn**. He *knew* the voice of his Heavenly Father. He *knew.*

So whatever the details of her past or present situation were, God led him to that park to provide a rescue for her. *That* he knew for sure.

Reeny, we need to talk." He was low toned and serious.

She set her coffee cup on the lamp table and scooted back on her bed enough to fold her legs underneath her comfortably. "I know. I owe you that much. Ask what you want to know."

He was considerately careful with his questions. He didn't want to upset her if he could help it. "Well, first off, you *owe* me nothing. I'm glad I was there to help you. Do you live here in Albuquerque?"

"Y…es." She hesitated. "I guess so."

"What do you mean, you guess so?"

"I did have a place…that…I lived. But I ran away a week ago. I guess I'm a little homeless at the moment."

"Where is your family? Mom? Dad? Husband?"

She shook her head and looked down at her hands folded in her lap.

Okay, he'd come back to that one.

"Reeny, who are you running from?"

Again, she didn't answer.

"Is someone trying to hurt you? Maybe someone driving a black Lincoln Continental?"

Her head jerked up, her mouth open in surprise. "How did you…know about him?" Panic swallowed her. "Who are you?" In a second she was on her feet, flight ready. One arm wrapped the bundle inside her belly as she whipped around and high-stepped one foot up on her bed to cross over to the door.

"Whoa, whoa." He was up and grabbed her around the hips, more of a protective move to keep her from stumbling and falling off of the bed.

When her feet snagged beneath the twisted bedspread, she and Donny both landed in a heap in the middle of the king sized bed.

So much for not upsetting her!

"No! Let me go. Please." Reeny fought like a prize fighter about to bring home the title.

His size and memory of the last bout he'd had with her helped him subdue her in two moves. Each hand wrapped a wrist, holding her arms above her head, as he slung one leg across both of hers.

"Get off of me you sorry…"

"Now, watch that name calling and settle down. I *do not* know who was driving the Lincoln. I only saw that car in the park about two minutes before I watched you make a run for my truck and hide. That's all I know. I swear, Reeny, I'm not here to hurt you."

When her muscles relaxed beneath him, he let go of her wrists and moved his leg off of her. They both continued to lie where they were.

“Now that we’ve established the fact that you know who was in that car, tell me about him. Or her. If I’m going to help you, I need to know what I’m dealing with.”

She closed her eyes against the hot tears filling them. If she told him who that was, he would leave. He wouldn’t want to help her anymore.

“Talk to me, Reeny Carr. Would that be Miss Carr or Mrs?”

“I’m not married.”

Why did he just sigh with relief? “Was that a member of your family?”

“No. He...he...” Reeny covered her mouth with her hand to quiet the cry coming up her throat.

He could already sense where this was going and felt a murderous anger boiling at whoever *he* was. He laid a calloused hand on her cheek and whispered, “I’m a big boy, Reeny. You can’t shock me. It’s not like I’m somebody special to you. You can tell me.”

She blinked away the tears and lowered her hand. Actually he was wrong about that. Thorn Brandon was *everything* to her. The one and only kind man she’d ever known, even though she had only known him a few hours since escaping hell.

She had thought living with her dad had to be the worst that was out there. And he wasn’t really her dad. He’d told her that a woman living with him for a while gave birth to her and then ran off and left her with him. Her name was Sadie and that’s all he claimed to know.

Harvey Carr. He'd raised her on whippings and very little food. She attended school through twelfth grade, threatened daily to keep her mouth shut and her bruises covered up—or else. She'd been too afraid to confide to her teachers. She didn't know the law would protect her from the abuse. And nobody ever knew what she endured.

The night of her high school graduation, she'd walked off the stage and was met by a strange man in the lobby of the auditorium amongst the crowd of grads and their families.

"Your father is waiting outside. He said to hurry it up." The man looked like a foreigner, maybe middle east.

She didn't wait around to ask questions, but hurried for the lobby doors before her dad had time to get too angry. She hadn't noticed that the strange man had followed her until her upper arm was grasped painfully and a fancy black car drove up beside her. Her assailant opened the back door and shoved her inside, getting in beside her. The driver took off without looking back.

She had been sold to these sick excuses for human beings and for the next year was forced into prostitution, kept prisoner in a tiny, filthy room somewhere in the same city. What she endured over the next months was something she would never speak of.

She had conceived a baby three months after being locked away, hiding it until she couldn't any longer.

Only one middle aged man, who she was told to call Sir, had paid for her exclusively during this time. When he finally noticed her body changes, he'd blown up in anger, bellowing that he would, *get this business taken care of right now.* He'd left her room in such a rage, he didn't lock the door. She ran.

She ran down a musty, rickety staircase onto the dark street. She ran around a corner of the building and headed for trees she thought she could vaguely see in the distance. She ran and ran until her legs gave way going down into a shallow ravine. There were trees and bushes and leaves. Limbs and dirt. Tumbling head over heels, she landed beneath some heavy foliage. The cold darkness closed in around her and she shut her eyes and curled her body up as tight as possible.

At that moment where she was curled up under the bush, a memory surfaced that had strangely come to her mind several times over her lonely, nightmarish young life. Mrs. Barnes, the middle school librarian, had told her about God, who's Name was Jesus. The only thing she could recall was being told that *if you ever need help, call out to Jesus and He will help you.* She really didn't know what that meant or who Jesus was for sure, but laying in the darkness under that bush in a pile of dirt and twigs and probably bugs, she tried it for the first time. It always sounded like a foolish thing. Tonight, she found it easy to whisper, "Jesus, if You are out there for real, I need help. Please." Then she slept warm and sound.

For five nights, she slept in that same hideout. During the day she watched from the woods along the perimeter of a park. Families picnicked and threw leftover food in the trash barrels. For three days she'd scavenged enough to get her by. She'd even found several unopened bottles of water that had been thrown away.

The third evening, the same black car that had taken her away on graduation night, drove slowly through the park. She knew it was Hasi, the scum that had shoved her into the car and locked her up in the upstairs room. She stayed hidden in the ravine for two days without sleep and with only a couple bottles of water to sip on.

During the third day, she felt an overwhelming need to go into the park. It was empty. She hid behind the base of a huge tree and became trapped there when a big truck drove in and parked just yards from her tree. A man in a black cowboy hat got out and stood beside his truck. She was so exhausted and weak, she knew she couldn't fight off an attacker, but she couldn't seem to hold still much longer either. Her feet wanted to run.

Just then, the black Lincoln showed up again and as soon as it disappeared further into the park, without thinking rationally, she ran for the cowboy's truck, grabbed for the door handle and jumped in.

She felt the callouses on his palm as they were sliding lightly back and forth on her soft cheek. It was the most soothing thing, his large, rough hand touching her so gently. She turned her face into his hand in response to her desperate need of this tenderness.

Without considering how she might react, Donny leaned in and lightly kissed her lips.

Her eyes grew as they stared and studied his. There wasn't any trace of a threat or violence that she was used to seeing on her dad and Hasi. And Sir. Thorn's face made her think of a child, sweet and innocent.

Reeny reached up and touched the soft smile on his lips. He kissed her fingertips. Their eyes were locked and Reeny thought this must be what love is like. Something sweet and compassionate, almost Heavenly poured into her from the deepness of Thorn's ocean blue eyes. She could have lain right there and never moved from his gaze for the rest of her life. She drank from a depth of human love so foreign, but so vital to her survival, now that she had tasted it.

"Thorn?" She faintly whispered. "Would you kiss me again?"

He leaned over and repeated his quick touch on her lips and when she pushed for more, he took her in his arms and pulled her closer, deepening the kiss.

He thought it might kill him dead, but he had to stop now before he got stupid. The blood was surging through his veins like a 747 on fire. When he pulled back slightly to end the kiss, Reeny grasped his shirt front in an attempt to pull him back.

"Reeny, let's sit up before we go too far." He pulled her up with him and caressed her face and hair. "We need to finish our conversation. I need some answers."

Her posture straightened and her shoulders stiffened along with her face expression. "Alright. He's a pimp called Hasi. He locked me in a room upstairs in some building and sold me for sex to a man called Sir. Sir came and went as he pleased and kept me locked in for the past ten months. My dad sold me to Hasi the night I graduated from high school. I figured he waited for that night so the school wouldn't be looking for me when I didn't come back. When Sir discovered I was pregnant, he got really mad and planned to kill my baby. He left and forgot to lock the door. That's how I got out of there."

Donny's mouth was open, his eyes huge, his heart cracking right up the middle at her unexpected and shocking answer to his last question. He didn't realize she had tears flowing until he snapped back from his dismay and heard her shrill, pain-laced voice.

"So you can get in your truck and leave now. I'll be fine from here." She didn't believe she would be fine at all, but his horrified expression told her this dream had just ended.

He couldn't move his eyes from hers. *Lord God!* He wanted to reach out and pull her back into his arms. He wanted to run out the door and find the dogs that did this to her and make them wish for death. Instead, he just kept staring at her. There was no move to make that would be the right one. *Lord?*

MARRY HER, THORN.

Those words rose up from the inside of him—from his heart, and they fell on his mind with such peace, and a yearning to obey. It hadn't been his imagination playing tricks on him. Not before and not now.

The thought of having this beautiful, abused, desperate, funny young lady to hold, to love, to show how good and fun life can be made his toes curl in his socks.

Then it hit him like a brick on the head. She was about to have a baby in two or three months. That thought settled inside of him with the same sweet peace that defies understanding. He would be her baby's daddy. Raise it like his own.

He didn't know *why* this all seemed okay. Like a good thing for him to do—a right thing. It was the only move he wanted to make now or *could* make. Something much bigger than him was in this and he understood what it was. He knew when the Lord was calling on his heart.

Just then, reasons to cut and run began to pop in his mind. They were both so young. How would he support a wife and child unless he took them home to High Point Ranch and continued working the dude ranch? Jesse definitely needed his help, even though he'd have cut out his own tongue before admitting that to Donny. Big brother wanted him in school, period.

And, he just possibly wasn't going to live long enough to worry about any of it anyway, because Jesse was going to kill him before he got to the ranch gate. And not only because he ditched college and hooked up with a strange woman who'd jumped in his truck uninvited, who was having a baby in a few weeks. Oh no, that alone wasn't enough. Nooo! He was also going home as *Thorn* Brandon. *Can anybody say Thank You, Lord!*

He let out a big sighing breath. Well, now that he had that out of his system, he pulled his attention back off of himself. This was about this young woman and an unborn baby. He needed to stay focused.

He reached out and took both of her hands in his. "Reeny, what happened to you—what was done to you, is not your fault. I think you must know that, but you have to know that I know that, too. You're as innocent as that little baby inside of you. That's how I see you. And more importantly, that's how Jesus sees you."

She inhaled sharply and tried to pull her hands out of his, but he squeezed tighter. Reeny wanted to tell him that she didn't want pity. That he didn't need to feel responsible for her just because she had picked his vehicle to hide in. But she was too broken, the lump in her throat too big to attempt to speak. Thorn's kindness to her in the face of what she was and her need of his brand of love overwhelmed her. She lowered her head and sobbed.

He didn't try to cajole her out of those tears, but stood and picked her up like he would have lifted a small child. Sitting back down on the side of his bed, he held her on his lap and laid her head in the crook of his arm, wrapping his other arm comfortingly around her. He held her like a mother would hold an infant and let her cry until she exhausted herself, knowing this wouldn't be the last expelling of so much layered pain that she would release. And he had every intention of being there to help her through it.

Both were finally quiet for a while.

"Reeny?" He said softly with his mouth against her hair.

"Hmm?"

"Do you trust me?"

When she didn't answer immediately, he asked again.

"Do you trust me?"

"Yes." The fact was, she felt safer in Thorn's arms than she'd ever felt for one day of her entire life.

"How would you feel about going home with me?"

"Where do you live?"

"High Point Dude Ranch in Jackson, Wyoming."

This brought her upright on his lap. "Wyoming?"

He nodded, giving her a minute to let that sink in.

"Is that where your family lives?"

"Just me and my brother, Jesse. We both own the ranch. And Jesse's wife and kiddos, too, of course. Then there are a few ranch hands scattered about. It doesn't get much better for a great place to raise a kid."

Her eyes darted a look out in space before bringing them back to his face. "Whose kid?"

"Any kid. But I'm thinking of yours right now."

"You mean, you want me to move in with you there?"

"Yes, mam," he answered without hesitation. "But we would have to make it right."

Her eyes widened on him with an expression of disbelief.

"I'll take care of you the best I know how and together we'll raise this precious little baby." He lay his hand gently on her stomach.

She couldn't speak or move through the shock that had temporarily frozen her brain. She just stared in complete awe of this unbelievable moment.

"Reeny Carr, will you marry me?"

***

CHAPTER THREE

A crisp early fall wind was blowing with skies that hinted snow when Thorn pulled up to the ranch gate and stopped just short of entering. The old saying, *there's no place like home,* rang loud and true in his insides.

He loved this ranch. He had no outstanding memories that came before moving here more than ten years ago to make his home with Jesse. Except memories of his mom and he didn't think of her real often anymore.

Martha Walton held a more prominent place in the maternal part of his life. Jesse hired her as housekeeper, but she became the female heart of the Brandon brother's lives quickly. From age sixteen on for Donny, she filled a mama spot, and brought a little respect for cleanliness and punctuality to both of the bachelor brothers. After she coerced the ranch cook, Hank Walton, into marriage a few years ago, in a way that only she could have done, the older couple filled out the Brandon's family in a wider circle of love.

But he wasn't sixteen anymore. And he didn't need a mom. He was coming back home after just a few weeks gone... as a man with his own family. He knew he had a tough announcement to make after he got up to the house. Normally when he'd had to face Jesse over an unpleasant issue, he'd swallow hard, his breathing would get shallow and he'd swagger in with a slump and get it over with.

He figured this was going to be worse than unpleasant, but there was a *standing up straight* feel on the inside of him that was strong and unbending. It was a strength that was beyond his own. One that spoke of a level of maturity that was so different from his loose, care-free way of dealing with life, especially as a teen growing up. And it also shredded all doubt that God was directing this show.

Jesse barreled through the back door, stomping and banging just a little too loud. Laura knew by that sound that something had him agitated.

She stepped back from the steam that was rolling out of boiling noodles on the stove and gave his noisy entrance her attention.

"Jesse?"

He jerked off his Stetson and threaded his long boney fingers through his thick hat-flattened hair. He replaced it and both hands moved to rest in the hip pockets of his work-dirty jeans. He shifted his weight onto one leg and stared down at the floor a few seconds.

Laura was feeling panic rise up. “Jesse, you’re scaring me. Has something happened?”

“That’s just it. I don’t know. Looks like I’m going to have to make a trip to Phoenix. Donny’s cell phone is turned off and I can’t get any help from the University. They said he wasn’t registered there.”

“Oh!” Laura reigned herself back in as quickly as she could. Donny had been gone a month. “When did you talk to him last?”

“The day he left for Arizona.”

“Maybe he’s just asserting his independence, Jess. Kids do that.”

He shook his head. “Not Donny. He’s never been that kind of kid. For all his joking around, he’s got a side to him that’s older than me sometimes. You know that, Laura.”

She did know that side of her young brother-in-law. The knot in her middle just got bigger, but she struggled to hold herself together for Jesse’s sake. “Well, let’s not jump to conclusions.”

“I’ll leave in the morning for Phoenix. Think you can hold the fort with these three kids.”

Laura nodded as she walked into her husband’s arms and held him tight. Words weren’t needed. She knew her man’s heart for the solid gold that it was. He loved his family with a fierceness that constantly threatened to crush his heart in the event of a tragedy. That fact scared her at times, but it was who

Jesse was and it was why she fell in love with him. In fact, it was Jesse who had shown *her* the road to love. And after three children and long days and seasons of running their dude ranch, they never moved out of the honeymoon stage of marriage. Not very far, at least. If two people were ever meant to be together on this earth, it was Jesse and Laura.

Their oldest son, Andy, was Laura's boy from her marriage to Matt Parker. She and Jesse married when Andy was five.

Laura was raised in extreme poverty with a bitter, cancer-ridden, reclusive mother. She'd been taught there was no such person as God and after her mom's death and her marriage to Matthew Parker, only the material side of life got better. She'd believed that was the good life on earth until Matt was killed and she and Andy met Jesse Brandon on a daring vacation to his dude ranch. She drove from Texas to Wyoming on nothing inside herself but determination. But she soon learned that the God who didn't exist had led her and Andy to a new life, a real, open, honest love of a God fearing cowboy, and to her invisible Heavenly Father Himself who had become more real than what she could see around herself.

Laura's gratefulness poured out into every person she encountered. She was determined not to forget where she came from or who had led her here.

Jesse showed no difference between Andy and his and Laura's two children, Anna Leigh and Jesse Dane, Jr. Andy was their first born, as far as Jesse was concerned and Andy seemed to accept that from the beginning.

SURRENDERED IV

Now, four years later, life at High Point Dude Ranch was like a mini Heaven to the Brandon family, complete with an adopted set of devoted grandparents, Hank and Martha Walton, a.k.a. Gramps and Granny, who were also the right and left arms of the service end of the business. The older pair always found time to haul the Brandon kids around like they couldn't get enough.

Life was good. Too good it seemed to Jesse as he held onto the woman made from his own rib, he was sure, and hated the fear that had sunk a fist into his gut. Just the thought of something bad happening to his brother was tearing at his heart. He fed on the power of his wife's strength at this moment as she silently gave him all she had.

"I'm flying out on the first jet to Phoenix in the morning. I'll call you as soon as..."

The back door creaked open just then and in poured three year old Anna Leigh with Gramps and Granny Walton on her heels. Hank's arms were full of one year old, Jesse Jr., until the toddler spied mama. Arms flailing toward her, Laura took the twenty pound load of wiggles off of the kid-whipped ranch cook.

"I believe we got em wore out for ya," said Hank.

Laura chuckled at that. "I'd bet an apple pie it's the other way around."

"Well now, might have to rethink that a bit. I *am* a little tuckered, now that you mentioned apple pie."

"Hank, that sweet tooth you got in there needs to come out." Martha jabbed Hank in the arm and laughed.

"Well, that would get just about all of em." Hank roared at his own joke.

Jesse and Laura both laughed as Laura set Jesse Jr. on the floor and got back to cooking supper. "You two hang around. This spaghetti will be ready in a couple minutes."

"Sounds good, but be sure you got enough in that pot. Saw Donny's truck there at the front gate when we came in," said Hank. "Had somebody with him, too."

Jesse jerked up straight and hesitated only a moment before his long legs made for the back door.

"Reeny?" Donny gently tapped his finger against her thigh. "Wake up, sleepy head. We're home."

She raised up and rubbed her face with both hands before she looked out the windshield to focus on the old west entrance gate. Two huge shaved logs stood like a regal welcome with a hand painted sign strung between them by two heavy duty chains. *High Point Dude Ranch* swung at least ten foot high in red lettering. Reeny felt her chest tighten with emotion. *Home. We're home.*

Thorn watched her take in the first sight of the ranch. Her eyes were lit up with a child-like excitement and he couldn't keep the grin off his face. "This is your home, Mrs. Brandon. At least, this is the gate into it."

It was that precise moment that it struck him for the first time, that he actually had no house to take his new bride home to. Jesse's family had grown until he'd moved his own bedroom into a makeshift space in a little side utility room off of the kitchen. That had been his idea because he knew he would be leaving for school soon enough. *Great!* The most he could hope for was an empty cabin this week. He knew they had all stayed full of dudes all summer.

Suddenly he found himself fighting inwardly with self-doubts. This marriage to Reeny seemed so off the wall at this moment. He wasn't prepared for this in the least way. What was he thinking? What was God thinking?

He heard it before he saw it. The whine of the ranch's golf cart was loud and coming on at a good clip. He figured Hank or Martha one would mention passing his truck at the entrance gate. And sure enough.

Jesse roared up to the driver's side of the truck and stomped the brake with all the anger that was triple-timing his heart rate. The glare he shot little brother abruptly mellowed out as his gaze fell on the young girl.

"Hello, brother." Donny's easy-going style didn't desert him. "Jesse, this is Reeny. Reeny, my brother, Jesse."

She smiled.

"Mam." Jesse tipped his hat and smiled, never short on polite respect for a female.

Donny spoke up before Jesse had a chance to ask any questions. "We'll be getting on up to the house. We can visit—at the barn."

Jesse nodded and eased the cart forward to turn around. *You better believe we're going to visit!*

"Lets start this with, what are you doing home and where have you been all month and why aren't you registered at college?" Jesse turned toward Donny in the middle of the barn alleyway, his hands squeezing his hips, his eyes blazing.

Donny stopped an arm's length from him and lifted his hat. His head itched something fierce and after killing a moment to ease that irritation, he settled the bent Stetson on the back of his head and spoke quietly, glad that Reeny chose to sit this out in the truck.

"Well, big brother, as hard as all this might be to explain, I'll give it a go."

"Big of ya," spouted Jesse.

He then related the last few weeks of his life as simply and detailed as he could, up to a point. He didn't quite get out the part about his name being changed or the fact that he had married the little stow-away. Or…that she was pregnant.

But that soon took care of itself when Reeny entered the dim lighted barn. "Thorn?"

Jesse's anger had subsided, engrossed with the intriguing tale. But the fact that she'd just called Donny by Thorn was more shocking than all the rest of the story. His face paled around a fresh angry scowl.

Donny wheeled around and walked to her, smiling. "Hey, girl." He reached for her hand and brought her alongside him and together they walked back to Jesse. Noticing her rounded belly, Jesse's mouth parted slightly.

"Jesse, this pretty little lady I've been talking to you about is no longer Reeny Carr. She's Reeny Brandon. My wife."

Jesse felt like he'd been hit in the back of the head with a shovel. The one that he was fixing to bury *THORN* with!

A time of stunned silence filled up the space around Reeny until a knot formed in her throat and threatened her air supply. The anger on Thorn's brother's face sent her backward a step. She wanted to run. Angry men were more frightening to her than being lost or alone.

Donny tightened his hold on her hand and stepped in front of her as a shield. He knew Jesse was scaring her. "Reeny's had a long day. She needs to rest. Reckon one of the cabins would do?" He stood up straight and stared Jesse in the eye. The stare was a courageous dare. Very quietly, without breaking eye contact, Donny's lips barely moved as he spoke with a tone of warning, "She's my wife."

Jesse was taken aback for a moment. He'd never seen this side of his little brother. Somehow in the month he'd been gone, Donny had changed drastically. At this moment, he seemed to have stepped into a man's boots. At least, he was trying on a pair.

Both men knew this conversation wasn't over, but they both needed a breather.

"Use the Hideout. Take her out there and get settled in. Everything you need is there. Food and bath supplies."

He nodded, turned and urged Reeny out ahead of him. In the truck, she sat without moving, trying the best she could to regain her composure. "What's the Hideout? Sounds like some place I would like."

He shot a glance at her face as he pulled away from the barn. She sounded like she was about to cry. "You'll love it. It's actually called *Honeymoon Hideout.* It's meant for newlywed couples, but sometimes older couples reserve it for anniversaries or just because."

She nodded and tried to swallow the lump in her throat before it produced tears, but she didn't make it.

He reached across the seat and rubbed her upper back. "It'll be okay, Reeny. I promise you, everything's going to work out." He turned his head and stared unseeing out his window as doubts suddenly shot into his head. *And you can promise her that because? Because God said so,* he shot back.

He drove through the open gate and headed down a well beaten trail across a few acres of pasture, then dropped off into a gully and back up the other side into the woods.

Reeny sat up straight, her eyes opened wide with wonder. Or was it alarm. When they rounded the last bend and stopped, facing the little doll house out in the middle of the most beautiful countryside she'd ever seen, Reeny couldn't keep from smiling. She'd never been out of the city like this. She had only seen pictures of woods, and open prairies, and little cabins beside creeks. She used to dream of living in just such a place. Riding a horse. Having a dog that would follow her every step. These were her dreams for so long. *Please don't let me wake up,* she begged whoever was the giver of her dreams. Because if she was only dreaming, she wanted to stay inside of it.

This was a new expression that Donny hadn't viewed yet on her face. He was held spellbound at the soft beauty that spread from her insides and coated her outsides. Even the light splash of freckles across her nose seemed to be dancing. He didn't know if he was actually in love with his little bride, but right this minute, he loved her. A gentle, unassuming spirit was easy to get close to. Not to mention, easy to please. This ancient, broken down little line shack, restored as a honeymoon getaway by Laura and Granny Martha a few years ago had captured many young lady's hearts. Who would have thought? And it appeared that the little cabin on the range had just acquired a new fan.

He grinned at her with that lopsided slant on his lips that was his claim to *lady-killin'*. Her eye caught it and flashed a tell-tale signal back at him. *Oh, yeah. Gets em everytime,* he gloated with all of the male ego this ranch could barely tolerate. "How about we go see the inside? You won't believe how these women dolled the place up in there." He got out and she eagerly scooted across the seat to get out of his door.

He led the way up on the small porch and pushed open the red door with a spray of yellow and white daises adorning the center of it. A small jagged piece of wood strung with baling wire hung across the center of the silk flowers. It read, *Honeymoon Hideout.* A flower box that stretched beneath the window sill was filled with various silk wild flowers.

Reeny was so taken with the storybook scene in front of her, she was caught off guard when her big rescuer/husband lifted her up in his arms and carried her through the doorway. He staggered after he stepped inside the cabin and groaned like he was trying to carry an extra heavy load.

"Thorn!" She latched on tightly and locked her arms behind his head. It got worse from there. One shoulder bumped against the door frame, then more groaning. Reeny was squealing. Finally, he teetered and swayed some more before he so carefully laid her on a bed. The death grip she held on his neck pulled him down with her, and when she let go, he kissed his little bride's open mouth before letting her go and stepping back, grinning with pride at his praiseworthy monkeyshine. He realized her squeals were actually laughter. He'd made her laugh and her giggles were still reverberating around the room. What more could a cowboy want in a woman?

He wanted nothing more than to pile up in the middle of that bed with her, but with more restraint than he thought he could muster at that moment, he stood still.

Reeny couldn't remember a time when a man had made her laugh and feel good. Thorn was so funny. She barely knew him, even though she'd married him. But she felt safe.

She sat up and let her gaze explore the interior of the cabin. She could view most of it from where she was. The kitchen had all the modern conveniences you'd want. A microwave, cook stove and refrigerator. Rough-hewn log benches stretched the length of an oblong cedar dining table. White ruffled café curtains hung over the small kitchen window. An old glass milk bottle filled with assorted wild flowers decorated the center of the table.

A fireplace filled the wall directly in front of the bed she sat on. A small red loveseat and cowhide rug took up the far side of the room, which was only a few steps from the bed and pots of artificial cactus and wild flowers filled the spaces in between. She looked down around her. This huge log bed's white fluffy bed covering and pillows was like sitting in the center of a cloud.

Donny was pleased at the delight on her face. This girl was a true cowboy's dream. Any woman's eyes that lit up with that kind of fire over a ramshackle hut and a few logs and frilly curtains had to have a cowgirl's heart lurking inside that skin. He had a strong feeling that he had the best part of this lady to yet discover. He just hoped the damage that had been forcefully inflicted on her young soul wasn't too deep to allow who she truly is, to fully surface. Regardless, Reeny Carr Brandon was his to cherish—for better or worse.

She looked up at him and something jerked deep inside her belly. She was sure the baby in there had nothing to do with it. Thorn's eyes were twinkle lights flashing at her. Humor and acceptance. Joy. Love? She felt herself being drawn straight into the silver blue sparks, calling her to come join them. Why? Why would this kind, very handsome man want her? She had been used like an old rag and was pregnant by an abusive old pervert. *Oh God. Oh God. Why?*

Donny watched her face change from the purest exhilaration to desolation in the space of a moment. She was looking at him when it changed.

"Reeny, what's wrong?"

She scooted to the edge of the bed and slid off of the side. She didn't realize how high the bed was until he grabbed her around her midriff and set her feet gently on the floor. She tried to step out of his grasp, but he held her in place.

"Reeny, talk to me." He knew some thought or memory from her past had just robbed her of this happy moment. "Tell me what you're thinking about?"

She turned her head and tried again to pull out of his hold, but couldn't. When she put one hand up, as if to hide her face behind it, Donny pulled her close against himself.

"Please let me go. I don't belong here." She fought hard to hold back the tears.

He held her tighter and pressed the side of her face against his chest. Her hand still covered her face.

"Reeny, honey, you listen to me. This ranch is your new home. You *do* belong here." He took her face in his hands and turned her to look up at him. "You're my wife. You're meant to be my wife. I wanted you to be my wife." He brushed his thumbs across her streaming cheeks. He didn't dare tell her that God had told him to marry her. "I know you hurt inside. You have a right to feel hurt and scared. But nobody will ever hurt you here. This is a safe place for you and your baby."

She stopped crying. He could tell she was hanging on to his every word, so he kept talking. "I know you don't love me. You hardly know me. And just because you're married to me doesn't mean you have to be a real wife. I don't expect anything from you. Nothing that you don't want. That you aren't ready for." He paused and searched her gentle, pain-filled eyes. "Okay?"

She finally nodded after a few seconds and he planted a kiss on her forehead and dropped his hands.

In less than an hour it would be dark, so he decided tomorrow would be soon enough to finish his and Jesse's conversation. But he did want to check on his old buddy, Trooper. That bay gelding was like family. He'd given Donny some of the best memories of his ranch life. Now it was time for him to make sure his devoted friend's older years were the best they could be.

Life changes for everybody as years roll by. Even names get changed. He knew he could ponder going from Donny to Thorn in the space of seconds from now until Jesus returned, and he still wouldn't guess the reason for it. So he simply settled himself to be Thorn Brandon, to Reeny, at least and let God be God.

"Why don't you get settled in while I get a couple chores done? The women around here keep this cabin full of food and drinks. Help yourself to it." He pointed toward a back room door. "In there is an old couch and the bathroom is back there too. I'll be back here before dark."

She nodded. "I can fix us supper. I'll do that while you're gone."

He smiled, that crooked grin automatically fixing itself on his incredibly sexy face. She knew this was going to be a long hour if she didn't get busy cooking.

He retrieved Reeny's two new carryall bags from the truck, along with his own bags, and set them inside the door before he left. He'd taken her shopping for jeans and tops, some maternity wear, shoes and boots and more personal items. The girl didn't have a stitch more than she was wearing the day she jumped in his truck, except for the things he'd bought her.

She headed for a hot shower first and put on the little dress Thorn had bought her their first day in the motel. All she could think about was how strong and safe his arms felt. They had shared the same bed every night they'd been together, before and after the justice of the peace pronounced them husband and wife. And not once had he even attempted to have sex with her. He'd told her from the start that he wouldn't touch her that way. Even after she became his wife, he had only curled her up in his arms at night and held her. She had worn the little dress every night until it had become a source of excitement when she put it on, knowing that soon she would be held tight and safe while she slept.

Reeny had never known what security felt like until Thorn. And that's all she wanted. The soft, easy feeling that his arms gave to her insides—Like nothing could ever hurt her or her baby as long as he was beside her.

All the ingredients were in the fridge and pantry for her favorite tacos. Thorn's oozes and ahh's over her first meal she made him was better than the spotty Christmas memories that she had clung to for so long.

Her dad would set a small tree on the only coffee table in the living room and at night he would plug it in and turn off all the other lights. He'd set her on his lap and tell her about Santa Clause and the reindeer. He even taught her to sing Jingle Bells. She could remember a big doll with dark hair sitting on the floor beside the tree and a small red wagon with a tiny little tea set in it. She was four or five then. She couldn't remember a tree or presents after that. She just remembered being hungry a lot. And hit. And shaken. And lonely.

"That was really good, Reeny. I've never had a taco made like that before, but I guarantee you could sell them."

"Thank you. I didn't create that recipe and I can't remember where I got it. I made it for me and Dad a lot." The spark in her face suddenly died away. Those memories made her feel sick, more now than before…before Thorn. Mixing even the simplest events of her past with the past few days of her life didn't mix at all. In fact, it magnified the horror of most of her life.

Donny got it. He seemed to be able to read this young girl, this stranger…his wife, with every mood swing that hit her.

He stood up from the table. "Go get some long pants on and your boots. And a jacket. We're going for a walk."

Reeny was ready in five minutes and headed out the door in front of him. Darkness had fallen, but a full moon had flipped a hazy light on. She stood on the ground in front of the cabin and stared at the tree line along the road and then beyond at the open field. She knew mountains lay beyond that because she'd seen them in the daylight.

He linked his arm in hers and headed quickly through the trees until there was nothing but open pasture in front of them. When he stopped, he looked back toward the trees with a panicked expression. "Thank the Lord, we made it. Never can be sure, especially in a full moon like this."

Reeny glanced back at the trees, then at Thorn. "What do you mean? We made what?"

"The little people. Surely you've heard about them."

"No. Who are they?"

"They're a tribe of *really* short people. *Really* short. And especially during a full moon, they hide in the trees and shoot arrows at you. Some of the Indian tribes around here say they're cannibals."

He crouched and glanced behind himself, then grabbed her hand and pulled her along at an easy trot, mindful of the extra passenger she was carrying. "Come on. I think I heard something back there." He was whispering.

"Thorn! You're an idiot." She knew he was playing with her. At least, she hoped he was.

"No, really. I forgot about the full moon tonight. That's when it's most dangerous. I better go checkup ahead. Wait here for me." He took off heading for the thickness of the trees without looking back.

Reeny looked around herself and quicker than she thought she could move, darted farther into the pasture to a boulder-sized rock. She squatted down behind it and waited. She spied a couple of small rocks on the ground, just right to chunk at a *little people.* Or better yet, at this slightly bow-legged comedian she had married. "Come on, buddy boy," she whispered. "Come to mama." On hands and knees, she stretched herself to peep around the rock toward the tree line. "You don't know who you're messin' with, cowboy. Come on. Show yourself."

When two large hands suddenly grabbed her around her semblance of a waistline and bellowed a war hoop over her head, she let out a real bona fide blood curdling scream of fear before crumbling in a fit of heart pounding laughter. Donny laughed until he had to sit down against the rock to catch his breath. When she sat up beside him, she punched him in the arm. "You're teaching this kid to be a mean pranster. He can hear all this, you know."

"Me! What was all that, *come on buddy boy, you don't know who you're messin' with,* business?"

"I'm just showing him how to defend himself."

"Really? Really?" He picked her up and set her on his lap in two easy moves. She squealed and giggled as he leaned her back in his arms and put his face right down to hers. "Go ahead, mam, defend yourself."

She got quiet and stared back into the glitter aimed at her. "I can't."

"Why can't ya?"

"Because…I like it just fine right here."

***

CHAPTER FOUR

Laura finished the supper dishes after Hank and Martha left for home. Andy took the children to the playroom and Laura headed outside to find Jesse. He never came back after heading to the front gate to meet Donny. She was concerned because Jesse never missed an evening meal with his family unless there was an emergency.

It was an hour after dark and the barn lights were all off. That was as rare as the fact that there were no guests at High Point this week.

She stood in the drive half way to the barn and listened. Only the rustling around in the petting zoo broke the total silence.

Then pup stuck her nose around the edge of the barn door into the fullness of the moonlight. Laura knew she would find her husband inside.

"Jess?" She called softly from the doorway.

There was no answer. She pushed the door all the way open and the stream of moonlight fell on Jesse's silhouette where he sat in an old ladder-back chair that was leaned back on two legs against the far wall. His head rested on the wall, his hat on the floor beside him. The look on his face was not one Laura had ever seen on him. His eyes were almost blank on the surface, but behind them, a storm was raging. She could feel it more than see it. She went to him and squatted down at his knees.

"Jesse, what is it? What's happened?"

He let the front legs of his seat fall back to the floor and then he leaned forward, clasping his hands together between his spread knees. He looked at the floor.

"Donny came home. Brought a young girl with him." He cut his eyes upward to look at Laura. "Says she's his wife."

Her eyes gradually grew wider. "His wife?"

Jesse nodded. "His *pregnant* wife."

It took her a long few seconds to find her voice. "Lord, Jesse. When…I mean, do we know her?"

He shook his head. "Never saw her before today." He paused a few seconds. "I've turned this every direction it can go and I can't make it add up. Hard as it is to think this way, I think Donny's lying."

"Lying about what, exactly?"

"I don't know, Laura. Part of it. All of it." Jesse snapped at her angrily. He jumped up, stepped around her and walked off a few steps. When he turned back, she stood up slowly trying not to take his outburst personally. "And that's not all." He stomped over and jerked his hat up off of the floor. "He's calling himself Thorn now. *Thorn*—for God's sake!"

Laura was understanding better by the minute why Jesse was fit to be tied. She'd seen him angry like this only once and that was before they were married. It was aimed directly at her when she and Granny Martha had given his old fashion dude ranch a more modernized facelift. It all washed well after the misunderstandings were cleared up. And it all worked out for the good. But for the life of her, she couldn't get a grip on how what Jesse was saying about Donny could have a snowball's chance at turning out for the good.

Donny, for all of his pranks and practical jokes around the ranch, was always one to count on in an emergency. He was always quick to act and make decisions when a situation called for it. The boy had been referred to as an *old soul* running around in a young body. Laura couldn't come up with rhyme or reason for this either, but she knew deep down, there had to be a plausible explanation.

"Where are they now? Do they need supper? I have plenty of spaghetti left. And what about. . .?"

Jesse put up a hand to stop her *mothering* from kicking in any further. "They're staying in the Hideout cabin. They're fine."

"Oh." Laura sighed. "I guess we'll get the whole story soon enough. Do you want supper now? It's my famous spaghetti, you know."

He didn't reply except for a quick shake of his head before he walked to the other side of the barn and out of sight.

She fought it, but wasn't entirely successful at keeping the stab of his words and actions from piercing her heart. Jesse's younger brother had been his whole life for so long. He'd raised him more like a father and son than brothers. And Jesse had plans laid out for Donny's education right from the beginning.

Donny had spent a little time in Phoenix a year or more ago. He'd visited the university then, but couldn't get settled on the idea of enrolling, so he returned home to wait one more year. Jesse hadn't been happy about that, and all but pushed him out the door a few weeks ago to get registered for the fall semester this year. And now this!

Laura swallowed at the lump as she went back to the house to get babies ready for bed.

Jesse hadn't taken Rebel Man out after dark for a joy ride in years. The full moon made a perfect night for it, although there was little joy in it for him. Rebel Man was feeling his grain though and Jesse held a tight rein until he reached the open field behind the barn. He knew every inch of the ground and tonight it was like riding in a lighted arena. When the pair reached a half mile straight away in open pasture, Jesse gave the stallion his head. Nothing could have soothed his raging mind better than the cold wind bathing his face from the back of his best four-legged friend.

Rebel Man had been given a miraculous healing several years ago, one that had brought him back from the brink of death. Jesse had been given the gift of his horse's life and Laura had seen with her own eyes just how real Almighty God is. Her atheist heart turned believer in the overwhelming display of God's power and love. Tonight, Jesse tried to bring back the memory of that moment as he sat astride his miracle pony, to let the anger and the hurt over Donny's escapade blow away. After a good ten minute run, Rebel Man was blowing as he walked it off. Jesse was still angry. Still wanted a piece of Donny Thorn Brandon's hide.

Jesse stepped down out of the saddle and loosened the cinch. He could see the Honeymoon cabin's lights through the trees. He led Rebel Man across the field wanting more than anything to finish his talk with his brother. Not tomorrow. Right now!

No sooner had that thought entered his head than he looked up and there he sat on top of the big rock in the middle of the pasture and looking straight at him. Even at a half acre away, the kid looked like a kid—tall and beginning to muscle up, but still Donny.

Jesse made his way to the rock, then pushed his hat back off of his forehead and looked up. "What brings you out this time of night? Marriage on the skids already?"

Donny ignored the sarcasm. "Heard a horse pounding the ground like it had something to prove. Thought one might have escaped it's pen."

Jesse settled his weight on one leg and fidgeted with the extra-long reins in his hand. "Think you might fill in some of the holes left in our conversation today?" He didn't wait for an answer. "Are you married to that girl in there?"

"Yes. We got a JP to do the honors."

Jesse looked at the ground and shook his head, then back up at his brother. "Where did you meet this girl, Donny? Obviously it was months ago."

"I met her a little more than two weeks ago in Albuquerque."

"Albuquerque. Two weeks ago." His jaw went rigid. It took more effort than Jesse thought he had to hold his peace. The scowl creasing his forehead deepened. He was fully aware that Donny was over twenty-one and his authority over him was expired. In fact, he'd always been proud of his young brother's mature and Godly way of handling his own affairs. Especially at his young age. In the important matters, he simply dealt with it and moved on. Where he could get by with it, he'd laugh his way out. He was a brand all his own. But regardless, he was still Jesse's *uneducated* kid brother who had better come up with a story to end all stories for this mess!

"Albuquerque, New Mexico is a far cry from Phoenix, Arizona. How in blazes did you manage that trick?"

Donny stared at the ground close to Jesse's feet, silently recalling the craziness of the story he was about to tell his brother. If he hadn't experienced it all for himself, he wasn't sure he'd believe it. But then again, it was just too far out there to have made it up. Even *he* couldn't concoct a tale like this one.

"Well, I was in a park. You know...parked...beside a picnic table and this girl ran out from behind a tree, jumped in my truck and I bought her a burger and a bed—you know, because she was hungry and tired and next thing I knew, we got married and here we are."

"Donny! I swear by all that's..." Jesse started forward and Donny threw his long legs over the top of the rock and jumped to the ground on the other side of it.

"Don't turn loose of that stallion, brother," Donny warned through barely suppressed laughter. "You'll be chasing him the rest of the night."

The two men had a stare-down over the top of the lone neck-high boulder.

"Honest, Jess." He couldn't keep the chuckle and smirk off of his face. "It's true. It happened just like that." Somehow it felt like filling in all the in-between facts would be easier now that the highlights were out there. But then, looking at the *you're a dead man* glare on Jesse's face...maybe not!

Donny put up a hand in surrender. He figured he'd gone far enough trying to lighten the scene. He knew Jesse was having a hard time with this. He wasn't real sure about it all himself. "Alright. Alright." He walked around the rock and leaned against it directly in front of Jesse. For the next twenty minutes, he told him the full story.

"And as quick as we left the JP's office, we headed for the ranch."

Jesse couldn't separate the emotional turmoil blowing his mind to bits. He was still angry, but wasn't sure at who. He wanted to beat the life out of Reeny's excuse for a father and words couldn't express his rage at the two devils that had kept her prisoner and forced atrocities on her little body that no one would really want to know the full extent of. His heart hurt for Reeny. An image of his own little daughter being hurt and degraded by such hellish monsters shot into his mind before he could stop it. Nausea waved at the murderous fury he felt at that picture. *And where were You, God? How many more Reeny's are out there screaming for help? And why Donny? Why tell a boy to abandon his whole future to support some rapist's child?* He couldn't stand it anymore. Without a word he turned around and cinched Rebel Man's saddle, climbed on and loped off the opposite direction from the ranch yard.

Donny's heart lurched in his chest as he watched him ride out of sight. He hated seeing his brother like that. He'd always been a strong tower for him to run to. He couldn't remember ever seeing Jesse in such a state. He took off his Stetson and with his chin crinkling, lowered his face. *Help him, Lord.*

"Get out of my way!" Clancy Bender shoved the smaller man aside as he barreled his way to the edge of the clearing. The full moon made it easy to watch the goings on around the little cabin that sat so perfectly isolated down below. "I say we head down there and get what we came for. The horse rider just took off and that other young cowboy won't be much to handle."

"No. No. Not a good thing to do now. Too much light tonight." Hasi was nervous and hated to be dirty or cold. And he was both. But more than that, he didn't like bloodshed or the threat of jail. He could jerk a young girl around and bully her better than anyone, but this was way out of his comfort zone.

Those cowboys were not small, weak looking men and he was afraid. He'd only come to this *wilderness* under threat of bloodshed…*his own*…if he didn't help Mr. Bender get Reeny back. Hasi believed, by all rights, he owned the girl, but Clancy Bender wanted her pregnancy terminated and Reeny back where she belonged. He'd teach her better about running off again. His money had bought and paid for her for a long time to come and he couldn't abide his money or his good name to be disrespected by a half-wit little whore. *No mam. She was gonna learn right off how to respect his authority.*

Donny turned up a small flame in the gas fire place before he slid under the covers beside his wife.

His wife. Those words had a different sound to them than they did yesterday. This pregnant little stranger was indeed his wife. The child in her belly belonged to a rapist. A child molester. A monster. He listened to her steady, even breathing as outrageous thoughts came out of nowhere to launch an attack against his mind. *This girl has been used and reused. She'll never function like a normal woman for you. She's emotionally cripple, sexually dead to a pure intimate relationship. Damaged goods. The sins of the fathers are passed down. This child will become like the father and there's nothing you can do to change that.*

He closed his eyes as a pang shot through his chest while the torment continued. *Look what you've brought down on Jesse's children. You've brought danger home to live and breathe in their midst.*

Where was this coming from all of a sudden? He got up quietly, redressed and left the cabin. At first, he wanted to walk. Then he changed his mind and got in his pickup and drove back toward the ranch yard, then out the front entrance gate.

Donny had never felt as helpless as he did this minute. Bile rose up in his throat until he thought he would be sick. Not once, since he'd first laid eyes on Reeny, did he believe he'd made a mistake. The past couple of weeks flowed by in such a state of peace. Then, wham! Nothing felt right.

Would God have allowed him to make a blunder this big and not warn him? Maybe He did warn him, but he'd missed hearing it.

He didn't blame Jesse for his feelings about this. Nobody in their cotton-pickin right mind would have done what he did— Right down to becoming Thorn. It all had felt so right. Marrying Reeny brought a joy into his soul. No regrets. No misgivings. And he wasn't sure that he was regretting it now. But every argument that had rushed through him as he had lain beside her brought a new line of reasoning to the whole circumstance. Did he bring danger right through the ranch gate? Through an innocent little baby that wasn't even born yet? Would Reeny suffer such emotional instability that she couldn't function normally?

Confusion took charge of his thoughts and he drove without a destination in mind. Soon he found himself on the main street of Jackson Hole.

His brows rose when he spotted Pastor Judd Luke's white dually parked in front of the popular Burger Gettin' Place. At least it *looked* like his dually. It seemed like a good time to visit with Judd, so he pulled in and parked in the only available spot a full block away. As usual, the place was busy.

When he got out, his gaze fell on the front end of a car that was backed up into a parking lot down the side street. A black Lincoln Continental. It was almost brown from a thick layer of dust. He shook his head. Of course, there *had* to be a car like *that* in town.

Inside, the lights were too dim and the room too packed with people to spot Judd easily. Donny took a seat at the far end of the bar, ordered a soft drink and scanned faces. Most were tourist. It appeared that the dually wasn't Judd's after all. He knew all the Double OO hands and none of them were there either.

He grabbed a package of peanuts and sipped his cola while George Jones put him in a more downcast mood than he'd come in with. *He Stopped Loving Her Today* moaned out of the jukebox until he couldn't take any more of it. The thoughts and fears that had taken over his mind earlier were gone. The torment was gone. He was left with a confused numbness. He wanted to talk to Judd Luke more than ever now, but it was getting late for knocking on a neighbor's door.

He took his time driving back home. A light snow was falling and as much as he loved the early fall snows, it didn't offer any help for his tangled heart. Probably for the first time in his life, he couldn't shut down the frustration of the idea that he may have made a monstrous mistake. Not just for his life, but for his family's.

It was pitch dark when Reeny opened her eyes. Something caused her to awaken suddenly, but she didn't know what. She listened for the sound of Thorn's breathing next to her, but the silence was as pure as the darkness in the room. She thrust her arm across the opposite side of the huge bed feeling for him, but he wasn't there. She turned on the dim light of the lamp beside the bed. The small alarm clock on the table showed almost midnight. He'd gone out to check on a possible run away horse, but that was hours ago. And what happened to the moonlight that poured through the cabin window earlier? She peered through the window, but couldn't see a thing, except blackness. She used the step stool to get down from the mile high bed and crept to the door and pulled it open. She couldn't believe her eyes. It was snowing. She stepped out to the porch rail and stuck her hand out in the gently falling flakes. It was like magic. She felt like she was standing in the end of the Cinderella fairytale. She, being Cinderella of course, had come through the rags and into her riches. She even had the glass slipper to prove it. Well—okay, she had a pair of very fancy, brand new western boots. But who's noticing? The only part missing was her prince. Where *was* her prince?

At the same time that it dawned on her the truck was gone, her bare feet began to freeze. She quick-stepped back inside and shut the door. A swift kick in her lower abdomen made her laugh. "Okay! Sorry." She grabbed a quilt off the foot of the bed and wrapped it around her middle. She was warm enough in her sweat pants and long sleeved t-shirt, but didn't know for sure if her baby could feel cold or not. The low blaze in the fireplace kept the small cabin comfortable.

With a steaming fresh cup of green tea and honey, she perched on the red leather love seat, her feet tucked up under her. She took in her surroundings more thoroughly, feeling like the most fortunate girl in the north. This tiny cabin held more beauty inside of it than any place she'd ever been in her life. She wondered how she had managed to survive her life. Most days, she didn't want to live to see the next. Many of those days were a blur now. Almost as if she had checked out in her mind while her body had been used like a trash can.

A television had been hooked up in her *prison* room and Reeny always regarded that little box of the outside world as her salvation. It was a toss-up between a Christian network and the Dr. Phil show as to who kept her sane. Maybe it was a combination, but one quote from Dr. Phil always seemed to come back to her, as it was trying to do now. It was something like *the abusive treatment of a child, changes who that child was to become. Bad things are written on the slate of that child's life.* Reeny grew up withdrawn and introverted. So who was Reeny Carr supposed to become? Was she even Reeny *Carr*? What did God have in His bag of plans for her from the beginning that she couldn't hope to accomplish now? Were Thorn and this ranch an alternate plan? If so, she didn't want to know any more. She couldn't imagine being with anyone except Thorn and she could hide out in this little dream spot forever. Nothing could be better than this.

But she couldn't help but wonder what the real Reeny was like. Maybe she was a boisterous loudmouth, laughing out loud at everything and nothing, like her high school gym teacher. Or a dare-devil, always quick to tackle dangerous stunts. A pioneer woman who preferred the outdoors? An actress? A singer? She giggled out loud. No, definitely not a singer. She had already listened to herself butcher that piece of artistry.

She sighed heavily and dismissed the wondering. None of that mattered now. She let her head lean on the back of the loveseat and closed her eyes a moment. She would sit up and wait for her husband to come home. That thought made her smile.

"What in blazes is this?" Donny hit his brakes and exclaimed his surprise at the two strange men on the highway just a few yards from the ranch gate. They were trying to flag him down. Of course they were. It was freezing out and snowing hard. He didn't recall passing a stranded vehicle from his direction, but they certainly needed help. He stopped and rolled down his window enough to talk. "Where you guys headed out here afoot?"

The bigger man leaned toward the window. "My pickup slid off the road back about a mile. Went right through a fence. A little light in the rear end, I guess. I'd sure pay you to run us back into Jackson Hole." He pulled a fifty dollar bill out of his wallet and dropped it through the window.

Sounded reasonable, for a couple of obvious tourists. "Sure. Hop in." Donny hit the door locks and in the next split second, his door was jerked open and two massive beefy hands grabbed him around the neck and choked him semi-conscious before reaching in to unsnap his seatbelt and jerk him out of the truck. The man slammed Donny's head against the door jam with such force that the motion of his head rendered him fully unconscious, even before the blow actually came. His limp and bloody form was shoved off the road into a growing snow bank. "Hurry up, man! Get in!"

His companion had frozen in fear at what he'd just witnessed. He figured the cowboy was dead and he would be charged as an accomplice to the murder. He ran around and jumped in. "We should get out of here. Out of this state. Tonight. We can get our car and be gone. No one will..."

"Shut up! I'm getting rid of that brat before I do anything else. And that girl—she's gonna learn to do what she's told."

The pair had already been out this way in a rented car the day before. Even drove right up into the ranch grounds, then back out after getting a good idea at how to get to the shack where Reeny was hiding.

"We couldn't a got a better break with that trouble-making cowboy showing up in town. Nobody seein this truck come in here will question us. Tinted windows can come in handy." Clancy Bender barked with laughter, and then choked on his spit.

Hasi would have gotten out and left the man to his dirty business except he was afraid of ending up like the dead cowboy. He knew Bender was pure evil, but he paid like clockwork in big bills. He didn't care what was done with the girl or her kid, but he greatly feared being locked away in a prison cell.

Bender drove slowly over the cattle guard of the entrance to High Point, spewing curses silently through his mind. Something about this place. Ever since he drove through the gate, he became more agitated, angrier than ever.

Hasi jumped and cowered when Bender's heavy fist came down thunderously on the steering wheel. His face was a frightening rage, his eyes bulging with hatred so intense, it even took the New Mexico small town Mayor by surprise. He wasn't sure why he was so furious. Things were working out well so far. Maybe it was at the audacity of that dumb northern cowboy showing up on his turf and butting in to business that wasn't his. He got what he deserved. And now she's gonna get hers.

Andy waved as his Uncle Donny drove past the barn and headed through the back gate toward the honeymoon cabin. The snow was getting heavier and Andy was checking on the petting zoo animals and worrying about his dad being out on Rebel Man in this snowstorm. His mom hadn't been her usual jovial self tonight. His eleven year old, going on twenty-five, antenna was up and he was concerned about the vibes he was getting.

He was known around the ranch as the resident care-giver. Always running around trying to make sure everybody's needs were met—people and animals alike.

Maybe Uncle Donny would know what to do about his dad. The intercom system in the house was on and he had overheard his parents talking in the barn earlier about him and his new wife. Probably he shouldn't bother them out at the cabin, but then, what if his dad was in trouble?

He snugged his knit ski cap down over his ears and fully zipped his hooded heavy down coat. His insulated gloves were almost too small, but they were better than the alternative. He set out walking to the Hide-Out.

"Coming?" Andy rubbed old Pup on the top of her head as he walked past her where she lay against the lamb pen. He and Pup had been inseparable the past six years, but his old friend's fifteen years were taking their tole. She usually opted for her rug in front of a fire these days.

Pup got up slowly on her stiffened back legs and hips and whined at Andy, but didn't follow him. She watched until he disappeared in the darkness, then ambled off in the opposite direction.

Cold had begun to penetrate the cabin and Reeny fiddled with the gas knobs until she figured out how to get a bigger blaze. She pulled her sweat shirt on over the top of her t-shirt and waited, worry building.

Maybe Thorn decided not to stay with her in this cabin. He would obviously have his own room in the big ranch house. He lives here. Maybe his brother, Jesse, had convinced him he'd made a mistake marrying her and bringing her here. Her heart fell at the thought. But she wouldn't hold it against either of them. God knew, she wasn't fit for decency.

The baby kicked her hard and she jumped, then laughed and cradled her abdomen. "Well, it's the truth, you know." Then she thought better of what she had thought about herself. "But you'll never know what kind of mama you have, little baby. I'm going to love you and be so good to you; you'll never know what kind of mama you were born to."

The sound of Thorn's dually made her jump up. Thank God. Quickly she smoothed the bed covers and fluffed his pillow before swooning toward the door. Before she got there, the door flew open with such force, she jumped and let out a startled cry.

The sight of Sir filling the doorway froze her blood. A good five seconds passed before her brain could tell her legs to move, and then she wheeled to run. Everything changed to slow motion. She couldn't get her lungs to breathe or her feet to obey the soundless scream that she could feel in her throat, but couldn't hear.

Clancy grabbed a hand full of hair and jerked her backward, catching her around the throat with his other hand. He didn't say a word, but hauled her outside and easily lifted her up to the opened truck door.

Wildness broke inside of her when she viewed the door as a cage. "Noooo!! Noooo!" She rammed her sock feet against the door jam on both sides and pushed herself backward. She twisted wildly, conscious of only one thing. The need to escape. The suddenness of her fight threw Clancy off balance. When he stumbled backward, she slipped from his hold and ran. There was a lot of yelling going on behind her. She kept running. One hand cradled her stomach—her socks were no protection against the rough ground. The darkness grew darker as trees grew thicker around her. She ran. She couldn't hear the voices anymore. She couldn't feel the cold air or the sticks and rocks bruising her feet. She was oblivious to everything except the urgency to escape. She continued to run blindly until her breath was almost gone.

"You stupid excuse for a human! You worthless scum!" Clancy shook an angry fist at Hasi. "Get out there and find her!" He grabbed Hasi by his shirt collar and dragged him out of the dually and shoved him into the dirty snow.

"I won't go to jail, Mr. Bender," came the high pitched fearful squeak. "You said you could take care of her yourself. You said that." The weaseling little man got up off the ground and worked at brushing himself off. "Anyway, she's as good as dead out there. She'll freeze and that kid, too."

After thinking for a minute, "Maybe." The thought seemed to calm Clancy's anger a little. "I want her found. I want to see she's dead." He stood there undecided what to do in the freezing cold and pitch darkness. The cold didn't stop him from going after her. But thinking of the dark folding in around him caused sweat beads to pop out across his wide forehead.

Finally, “Get in. Let’s get back to the car and ditch this truck. We’ll wait up on the ridge til light.”

When the truck backed up to turn around, Andy hunkered down behind a big aspen and sucked quick shallow breaths. He’d run most of the way after hearing a woman scream and stopped just out of sight when he saw a large strange man fall backward in the melting snow. The woman ran towards the trees. He only heard the rest of it. *Mr. Bender.* He’d never heard that name before. *Where is Uncle Donny?*

The dually went past and after a few seconds, Andy stepped onto the road. He hesitated a moment about which way to go, and then ran to the Hide Out and stepped inside the open doorway. A loud clap of thunder made him jump and duck.

“Uncle Donny?” There was no answer. He spun around and raced into the darkness the same direction he’d seen the woman go just as the light snow turned into a blinding deluge of ice cold water.

***

CHAPTER FIVE

Jesse stomped and raked his muddy boots outside before leaving them to dry just inside the back door. He padded down the dark quiet hallway to the shower, and then found Laura propped up on pillows in bed pretending to read a book. He stopped just inside the bedroom, most of his anger mellowed. He knew he had hurt his wife's feelings earlier.

He cleared his throat. "That, um, crap out in the barn earlier was uncalled for."

She cut her eyes at him. Curse words were a rarity for Jesse, but she knew he was battling some intense anger and hurt. "Yes, it was."

He looked at the floor and bobbed his head up and down. "So…am I still invited for supper?" His stomach felt like it had gone into starvation mode, gnawing on its own self.

It rankled her that he would suggest she get up and feed him now. "Of course. But the cook's off duty. Help yourself." Her tone was enough sarcastic to resurface his bad mood.

"I'll do that," he smirked. "So why are half the lights in the house still on? I thought we agreed to watch leaving unnecessary…"

"Andy is still up, Jesse," she snapped. "He went to check the barn."

Jesse stopped and blinked a couple of times. "I didn't see Andy when I put Rebel up. Come to think of it, the big lights were burning in the barn when I got here."

He turned toward Andy's room and opened the door. The light was on, but Andy wasn't in there.

He checked Anna Leigh and Jesse, Jr.'s beds. They were asleep.

He headed to the back door with Laura on his heels. It was raining so hard now, they could barely see the barn. Jesse had flipped the lights off out there and they were still off.

Laura attempted to push past him and go out, but Jesse blocked her.

"You can't go out in this storm. Check and see if Pup is in the…"

Just then, Pup appeared at the back door drenched and shaking and whining. Jesse opened the door, but Pup uncharacteristically stepped back into the rain, still whining.

She started to leave, then stopped and barked back at Jesse before trotting off down the drive.

Jesse sensed the dog knew something that he needed to know, too.

"Stay here, Laura. I'll see where Andy's hold up. Probably the barn." He didn't bother with his rain slicker, but stepped into his wet boots, sliding the bottoms of his sweat pants inside, jerked his coat on over his short sleeved t-shirt and ran to the barn.

Sixty seconds inside told him Andy wasn't there. He ran out to his dually and headed off in the direction he'd seen Pup go. With his wipers and headlights on high, he still couldn't see but a few feet out in front. He stopped at the road just past the cattle guard. No sign of Pup. This was crazy. That poor old dog had probably gotten senile and didn't know where she was.

He turned onto the highway and stopped to back up when Pup appeared in the lights. She was barking frantically at the truck, then turned and disappeared. Jesse figured he'd better try to take her back to the house with him. He drove that direction slowly and scanned the sheeting darkness.

Come on, old girl. Where'd you go?

Then he spotted what looked like her, curled on top of a rock or...something. He pulled up alongside and pushed open the passenger door. Before he could call out to the dog, he recognized what she was laying on. A body!

Andy! God no!

He lunged across the seat nearly falling out and scrambled across the shallow ditch. Pup had moved and Jesse grabbed the limp form, too big for Andy, and gently rolled him over. A strangled cry rang out. Jesse didn't realize immediately that it came from his own mouth.

"Donny!" Jesse put his ear against his brother's soaked chest and felt his wrist for a pulse at the same time.

He's alive! "Donny!"

The side of his head was bloody and swelled. Scrambling into position on his knees, Jesse pulled him to a sitting position and then immediately frontward to hoist him over his shoulder.

Fear and adrenaline worked wonders for extra strength. He lowered him onto the front seat and curled his long legs in after him, then opened the back door and scooped up the wet, cold Pup and settled her inside.

Within the hour, Donny was in the Jackson hospital ER, conscious, but not making much sense. Jesse phoned Laura to tell her where he was, and then learned that Andy still hadn't shown up.

"Stay inside and lock up. Don't even think about... Laura?" He heard a dial tone. "Crap!"

Leaving his information at the ER desk, he raced back to the ranch. Andy was still missing and if he didn't hurry, his wife would be, too. He hoped she could think straight enough to not leave the two babies alone in the house. Her mama's heart had a stronger beat to it than any he'd ever seen. Maybe all mama's were like that, but this one was *his* wife and the mama of *his* babies. *Lord, my family is falling apart around me. I could use some Help here.*

Jesse squinted his eyes, watching the road directly in front of his truck. The rain was relentless and just a little more of it would undoubtedly cause some serious flooding. Only once since he'd owned High Point Ranch, had he seen the creek overflow its banks. It had been impassable for days, but there was nothing on the other side that mattered. The ranch was sitting on higher ground.

Lightening crackled across the sky in front of him and he sped up. Hopefully Andy will have shown up by the time he drives in.

This night was nothing short of a nightmare. What had happened to Donny? Where was his truck? Where was Andy? And this *wife* of Donny's. Did she have something to do with his being hurt?

He slammed his fist on top of the steering wheel. *Where was that boy's head?* He could see his sensitive little brother picking up a hungry stray dog or giving an elderly person a ride. Or letting a hitch-hiker pile into the bed of his truck. But marry a pregnant prostitute because she needed a baby name or a sugar daddy or…or because she stowed away in his truck? *This is great, Donny Brandon! Just great! This stunt just may have cost you your life!* "Damn it!" He pounded another lick to the steering wheel. "Damn it!"

Somewhere deep down, he knew he should repent for cursing. Repent of this anger he harbored for the little pregnant girl that had barged into his family's placid life on the ranch, staking a claim through the Brandon name. But he was too angry to follow through.

Reeny had put every ounce of strength she possessed into running and not looking back. Even though the trees were dense and dark, the sound of the storm's hard pounding rain was thankfully relentless. She figured that noise covered up her own.

But suddenly there was a different sound. It was water, but more than rain. She was running through nearly knee high creek water, but stepped high and kept going, running blindly through the darkness.

When she reached the embankment on the opposite side of the creek, she tripped trying to step out on the soggy sand. Her knees hit the ground hard and before she could scramble to her feet, she heard a voice almost directly behind her.

"Mam? Mam?"

She couldn't stop the frightful cry that shot up her throat nor did she attempt to slow down. The voice had sounded like a child, but that wasn't possible. It was *him!*

She couldn't get her feet solidly under her. She was trying too hard.

"Mam?"

"Oh, God!"

Hands were on her upper arms from behind her while she kept plugging to get up.

"I'll help you. The creeks gettin' up."

"Let go of me!" Reeny screamed and fought until she felt her fist connect with Sir's face.

"Ow."

She saw him now as he slid in the mud and landed next to her. His head was covered with his coat hood. She saw him swipe a gloved hand across his smarting jaw, but he wasn't Sir. She froze. He was a kid—A young boy.

"Who...are you?"

"Andy Parker. I saw that man try to kidnap you. I was afraid you'd get lost. I came to help you."

Just then, the creek water rose rapidly at their feet and the rain came harder. They both got to their feet.

"I know a place we can go. It's right up there." Andy pointed straight up and it was the first time she realized there was a virtual cliff directly in front of her. "We have to climb up to it."

"Okay."

Reeny followed right behind Andy, stepping in his boot marks. On the way up, she felt the cold freezing rain for the first time. Her teeth began to chatter and she had a hard time grasping onto the tree limbs and rocks. Her hands were freezing.

Finally, they reached a short ledge. Andy reached for her arm and pulled her the last step up. The mouth of a cave stood open in front of her. The only way she could get the nerve to go inside was because her young rescuer had gone ahead of her.

It was blessedly dry inside, but so cold. Her clothes and hair clung like a second skin. She remained just inside the entrance. It was pitch black, but she could hear the boy making noise just beyond her.

In an instant, a small light penetrated the dark interior. Andy looked up and her heart squeezed at how young he actually was. Ten or eleven?

"I have some camping stuff in here. I come here sometimes. I can make a fire."

She watched as he busied himself getting dry sticks and chunks of wood from against the cave wall. It looked like a black plastic bag that he dug around in, finally producing a lighter and a wad of paper towels.

Presently the blessed warmth of a fire lighted a welcome off to the far side and just inside a second smaller concave. She had to walk fully in and look around a rock wall that jutted out just far enough to conceal the flickering blaze.

Andy looked at her and recognized the fact that she was going to have a baby and that she was shaking really hard.

"You can come over and get warm," he offered shyly.

Reeny felt like crying with relief as she sat beside the blaze. But for the boy's sake, she smiled instead. "Thank you, Andy Parker. You saved my life. I'm so sorry I hit you. I thought you were…that man."

"It's okay. It didn't hurt much. I have some old blankets I camp with in the bag. You can use them." He walked over and pulled two large blankets from the bag and handed them to her.

She pulled her soggy sweatshirt over her head and wrapped one blanket around her soaked t-shirt clad upper body.

"You should pull off your wet coat and wrap up in the other one, Andy. It looks like we might be here all night."

He did as she said and sat down across the camp fire from her.

"So where did you come from, anyway?"

"I was coming to get Uncle Donny. My dad was riding his horse out in the storm and he didn't come back. I thought Uncle Donny would know what to do."

"Is Jesse your dad?"

"Yes, mam."

"But your name is Parker?

"Jesse's my step-dad."

"Oh."

"Those men were in Uncle Donny's truck. Did they steal it?"

Reeny's eyes widened with alarm. She hadn't realized that fact. "I don't know. I don't know where Thorn, um, your Uncle Donny went."

Now that she knew Sir was driving Thorn's vehicle, she began to feel sick. He must have seen her with Thorn back in Albuquerque and followed them. *Oh please no. Please God, don't let Thorn be hurt."*

It dawned her then that he'd said *those* men.

"How many men were in the truck, Andy?"

"I saw two."

Hasi.

"How did you run through these woods without them seeing you?"

He shook his head. "They didn't run after you, Miss ...um...they drove back out."

Her eyebrows went up. She was surprised and relieved, but sick almost to nausea, worried about Thorn.

"That's good. I guess we should try to sleep the rest of the night. And, by the way, I'm Reeny."

Andy stared at her a moment before his curiosity got the better of him. "Are you married to Uncle Donny?"

She nodded. "Yes, I am."

A slight smile pulled his lips. "I'm glad." He lay down and curled up under his blanket.

She followed suit.

Reeny was exhausted to the point of sheer weakness, but the cold and the pain kept jerking her back from sleep. She dozed again, but finally the pain was too great to ignore. A loud wail echoed off the rock and dirt cave walls, bringing both her and Andy to sit straight up.

Andy jumped to his feet and Reeny doubled over grasping her stomach. "Oh, it hurts!"

Andy ran and grabbed more wood to build up the small blaze. Listening to her panting and almost screaming, he knew. He squatted beside her and pulled the blanket back over her shoulders.

"Is it time for your baby to come?"

"I…oh oh…I think so. Oooh! Not now. Please not yet," she moaned.

Andy got his blanket and draped it around her on top of the other one. "I have to go get help."

The contraction subsided. “No, the creek is too high. Andy…ow…oooh…oooh. God…Help me!”

Her high pitched scream was horrifying to Andy’s young mind. Without another word, he jerked on his wet coat, knit cap and gloves and ran to where the trail started downward. He could hear water rushing, but couldn’t see it in the darkness. Regardless, he had to make his way to the ranch in a hurry.

The trek to this cave and back was one he could do with his eyes shut. He’d discovered it scouting around one Saturday morning. He hadn’t told anyone about the cave because it was nearly a mile from the ranch and outside of the range where he was allowed to wander alone. It had taken him several trips to get a store of firewood and kindling and his other camping stuff up the side of the cliff, never suspecting how it would be used for an emergency like this. He could be feeling real proud of himself, but at the moment, he just felt desperate to get help for Reeny.

The rain had stopped but the creek was moving fast. He had to cross over. He could swim, if necessary, but suddenly he felt afraid. He knew how powerful this kind of water could be. If he didn’t make it, he could hardly stand the thought of how sad his mom would be. But if he didn’t try, Reeny and her baby might die up there. He had to try.

Carefully he stepped into the swirling creek in the same spot where he always crossed. The waist high water was freezing, but he leaned as hard as he could against the current and headed for the opposite bank. Even though he couldn’t see, he kept his eyes trained in the direction of his destination.

Not far now. Almost there.

"Ahh!" A shrill yelp leaped from his throat when something rammed into his upper body and knocked his feet out from under him. The swift current rolled him under for a few seconds until he grabbed onto the dark, invisible monster that was all over the top of him.

A tree limb. It's a tree limb."

He grabbed for a better grip and held on while he was dragged through the swift flood waters. When the tree lodged solidly into a pile of brush, he was jerked to a quick stop, almost losing his grip. He could see enough to realize he was still out in the middle of the rolling creek. Tightening his grip, he knew he had no choice but to wait. And pray.

Jesus, I'm really scared. Please send some help for Reeny and her baby. And for me. Thanks. Amen.

The rain had let up by the time Jesse reached the ranch. He practically ran through the back door.

"Laura?"

They met in the hallway just as she rounded the bedroom doorway. Fully dressed for outside, she grabbed Jesse around his middle and he pulled her into his arms.

"Okay. Hang on." He hugged her up against him feeling some of his anger recede for the moment.

"I can't find him, Jesse. I can't find Andy. Hank and Martha are coming over to stay with the babies. We have to go find him." She tried to pull away to head outside, but Jesse held her. She was working herself into hysteria.

"We'll find him, honey. I'm going to call for more help. Judd Luke will get his hands to help search." He jostled her with his arms still penning her against him. "Promise me you won't run off out there. You'll wait for me to make this call."

She nodded and he released her and headed for the office down the hall.

The back door slapped shut and Martha Walton made a bee line across the kitchen floor to reach Laura with a quick hug. "Andy's fine, honey. I know he is." She turned and headed toward the counter across the room. "I'll make a pot of coffee."

Hank stepped inside the kitchen. He held the storm door open a few seconds looking outside, then closed it and turned to Jesse who had just entered the kitchen carrying his heavy coat.

"Hank. Martha. Thanks for coming over," Jesse said. "I'm figuring Andy's hold up out of the storm somewhere. Maybe he fell asleep. Judd and a few of his boys are coming to help look for him."

They were all staring at him. Jesse didn't realize the short, angry sound of his voice or the intense scowl creasing his face. He slid his coat on and zipped up.

He darted a glance at Laura. "Donny's in the hospital in Jackson. He got hurt. Don't know how yet, but as soon as we locate Andy, I'll head back to see about him." He deliberately left out the fact that Donny's truck was missing.

"Think maybe you should call the law?" Hank asked. He sensed there was more to all this than Jesse was telling.

"Already did that from the hospital. They'll be there waiting to talk to Donny. Let's get Andy rounded up first, then we'll figure that out."

Jesse headed for the back door. "All of you stay here. One lost out there is enough."

"Jesse, I let your dog out of the truck," Hank said. "She was having a fit. Couldn't get her to come inside, though. She seemed kinda nervous. Guess I could check on her right quick."

Jesse hesitated only a moment before what Hank said fully registered. He hurried out the door into the chilly, wet night and scanned the grounds.

"Pup! Come here, girl." He called to her a couple more times, before turning to Hank who had joined him.

Laura came out behind Hank.

"Did you see which direction Pup went?"

He waved his arm. "Off that way. She was sniffing the ground and whining like she was on the hunt."

"Stay here. You too, Laura," he yelled as he took off with long strides toward the barn. Headlights rolled over him before he got there and he waved the vehicle forward without turning around.

-336 Judd Luke pulled his dually in at the barn. Six cowhands, plus Les Kane and his wife, Kaitlyn, unloaded.

Jesse filled them in and sent a couple men to search each cabin and teepee in the camp ground.

"Kaitlyn." He nodded respectfully. "You're welcome to wait at the house."

She shook her head. "I came to help search."

"Jesse, was Andy upset about something?" Judd asked.

"No. He came out here to check on the zoo animals before bed and never came in. And now, Donny's in the Jackson hospital. Looks like somebody roughed him up pretty good and stole his truck." Jesse filled them in on a little of Donny's escapade, leaving out the extremely personal parts. "So he brought home a bride. They're staying in the Honeymoon cabin for now."

Judd lifted his Stetson and repositioned it. "Do you think Andy's situation has anything to do with whatever happened to Donny?"

Jesse shook his head. He was at a loss for *what* was going on. But he didn't like the fear that kept trying to creep up his spine. Something was wrong. He just didn't know which way to go first.

When the search of the campground came up empty, Jesse decided to head out to the cabin and check with Reeny. Judd, Les and Kaitlyn went with him. One man was posted as a guard at the house and the others spread out five different directions.

The cabin lights were on, but the front door was wide open. One quick check inside and Jesse's alarm flags began to fly high. The cabin was empty, but the muddy foot prints half way into the front room set off an alarm in all of them. They were very large shoe prints.

There was still no sign of Pup. Could she have gone to where Andy was? She only went as far as the barn and back to the house these days. But Pup had been Andy's sidekick since he was five years old.

Jesse called out into the blackness. "Andy! Pup!" He didn't believe for a second anyone was out there, but he called anyway. "Reeny!"

Everyone held their breath and listened.

Judd put a hand on Jesse's shoulder. This didn't look good. "Let's get some sheriff's deputies out here."

Jesse's emotions were trying to get the best of him, as it was, but his friend's gentle gesture almost broke him. The preacher was as tough in the saddle as any one of his ranch hands, but he had something else working on the inside of him that showed clear through his eyes and sounded in his voice. It was genuine kindness with no strings. There wasn't any prideful holier-than-thou churchliness in the man. It wasn't something that could be imitated either, because there were times when he tried to be more like his pastor friend. And he always failed. Even miserably, like now.

This thing with Donny and this girl seemed to have cracked open something inside of him that he didn't know was there. And now his brother is hurt and his son is missing and still he can only shake the anger that's chewing him up, for moments at a time. He's acquired a whore for a sister-in-law and if anything has happened to Andy or Donny because of her...

His mental raging screeched to a halt when he heard something. They all heard a dog barking off a distance toward the creek.

"That's Pup!" Jesse shouted as he headed off at a run.

Flashlights shot into the darkness as Kaitlyn grabbed a heavy wool blanket out of the back seat of the truck. They followed Jesse, running as fast as the mud and trees and thick undergrowth allowed. The barking was loud now and so was the flooding creek.

"An-dy?" Jesse yelled and the barking stopped.

Within seconds, Pup appeared out of the darkness, soaked and muddy. She whimpered and turned back toward where she'd come from.

The group tore through the dense woods reaching the flooded creek.

"Da! Dod!" Andy could barely get his frozen mouth to cooperate. He heard his dad calling his name and he could see streaks of light darting along the creek bank.

"There he is!" Les pointed toward the pile of brush in the middle of the widened creek.

Andy had climbed up out of the water and was hanging onto the highest limbs from a dead tree that had washed down. It appeared that the creek had been a lot higher out of its banks than it was now and was receding quickly.

Jesse walked into the swirling water stepping carefully to gage the depth. It was hard to tell in the dark, but he reached Andy without getting much deeper than his knees. He grasped the shivering boy under the arms and lifted him up and out of the tree limbs. Ordinarily, he couldn't have picked him up that way now. Andy was getting to be a good sized boy. But adrenaline is a powerful thing—a gift of God when extra strength is needed. Like when you're scared out of your mind that your boy's life is on the line. His brain said to scream at the kid and demand answers, even though Jesse had never raised his voice at Andy for any reason. But his daddy-heart was pounding with relief and fear and with strung-out emotions over the recent sight of his young brother lying bloody in a ditch and now his son in freezing flood water that it was a God's wonder he was found.

Jesse carried his cold, soaked and scared boy like a small child riding his hip, back toward the bank. Les and Judd had waded part way out and took him from Jesse. Kaitlyn wrapped the blanket around him while they sat him on a fallen tree log.

Les squatted in front of him to look into his face for signs of shock and check his vitals the best he could. He seemed alright for the most part, but all agreed he should be checked at the hospital ER.

"D...Dod...up ther." Andy tried to tell them about Reeny, but his lips were too stiff and cold to form his words.

When Jesse tried to pick him up again, he fought him off and tried to talk again.

"Reni. Baby." He waved his arm and pointed up the creek, knowing the water had washed him down a good ways.

"Son, are you saying Reeny? Did she have something to do with you being out here?" Jesse bellowed.

He nodded his head up and down.

Rage raced through him. He knew it! That girl brought destruction right into his house.

Finally, Andy began to rally and stood up. "Up there." He pointed again. "The cave. Her baby is being born. I was t...trying to get help, but the water..."

Les took Andy by the shoulders. "Okay, slow down. Somebody is having a baby in a cave?"

"Reeny is. I'll show you." Andy took off holding the blanket tightly around himself.

Cave? Jesse took off behind Andy deciding it was just possible he could wake up any minute to find this was one of those hair-brained dreams people get sometimes.

"Donny."

The feminine sound calling his name was familiar. He had awakened in the hospital with tubes in his nose and needles stuck in his wrist. He glanced at the closed mini blinds that covered the windows and could tell it was dark outside.He didn't see anyone in the room, then he supposed he went back out for a while.

"Donny."

This time he came fully awake and pushed himself up to sit on the side of the bed. He felt perfectly fine and couldn't seem to recall what had happened that landed him in here. He put his feet on the floor and stood. He thought he should feel pain or dizzy from some kind of injury. Instead, with the tubes and needles gone now, he felt better than he ever had in his life. Even the loose fitting gown they had put on him was a pleasant thing to wear. But he didn't want Jesse to see him in it. He'd never let him live it down.

In the next instant and as simply as drawing in a breath of air, the atmosphere changed. He was outside...somewhere, standing in a brilliantly lighted meadow. It was like very bright sunlight, only different. It wasn't blinding. It was soothing. He looked down at himself and he was still wearing the hospital gown. The hem was past his ankles, but didn't cover his feet. He was barefoot. The ground he stood on looked like regular ground, but it felt like silk under his feet. The grass was a deep green that was so animatedly beautiful, he decided right then he was having a dream.

Slowly he raised his head and looked across the field of green and could hardly take his eyes off of the multicolored wild flowers that poked their various shaped heads up through the grass. Nothing could compare to the beauty of this meadow. He fought an overwhelming desire to lie down and roll around in it, but restrained himself only because he didn't want to crush the flowers.

Music sounded from somewhere, and yet it seemed to be coming from *every*where. The flowers at his feet seemed to be singing. He looked down again and that's when he saw that there were flowers under his feet, except they were not broken. They actually were standing straight and tall right through the middle of his feet.

He jerked his hands, palms up, to look at them. They looked normal. He wiggled ten fingers, but the sleeves of his gown, that he just noticed was brilliantly white, came to his wrists.

Immediately, somehow, he knew. *I died. I'm in Heaven.*

And he also realized that he was perfectly alright with that. Better than alright. He was filled with an excitement beyond his capacity to understand. He simply felt like running and jumping for pure joy.

"Donny."

He knew the voice. He remembered it from so long ago. At the same moment that recognition came, she appeared in front of him. And the next instant, he was in his mother's arms. Tears spilled down both of their cheeks, but they were happy tears.

"Mom, you're alive. Alive. I missed you so bad."

Her laugh was filled with merriment. "Yes, I'm alive, my boy. My beautiful boy. Everything here is alive and filled with our Lord's Glory."

He was filled with questions, but before he could formulate even one of them, his thoughts seemed to be cut off. His mother became quiet and a little stoic. She turned slightly and gestured with her hand and Donny looked that direction.

Reeny?

***

CHAPTER SIX

The group reached the creek crossing below the cave just steps behind Andy. He could tell the water was closer to normal and never slowed down when he got to the bank.

They all plowed across the, knee-deep flow, but when Andy grasped a tree limb to begin pulling himself up the cliff, Jesse grasped his arm.

"Whoa, Andy. What are you doing?" He was afraid his son was hurt and not thinking clear.

"The cave is up there, Dad." He reared back and pointed straight up.

They all stared upward, almost the same dumbfounded expression coating each of their faces. Nobody moved until Andy dropped his blanket wrap and vanished up the slick side-winding trail.

Les Kane was the last to be helped over the top of the ledge before they all rushed inside the wide opening of the cave. They found Andy standing a couple of steps from the girl as if frozen in place.

It was Les who reacted first, after the initial shock loosened that had struck the whole atmosphere inside the cavern. It didn't matter that he was a veterinarian. His doctor's instinct rushed him to her side and checked first for a pulse. He couldn't find it. Judd went to his knees beside Les and began to pray quietly for the girl's life. Kaitlyn gasped and knelt beside Judd, silently joining his prayer.

Reeny's small body was partly curled in a fetal position. Her long blonde waves splayed over her face and across her bare arms like thick silken strings. She only wore a thin long sleeved t-shirt, her knit jogging pants pulled down to her knees. Mud and blood lumped together on her clothes and the ground around her. A dirty blanket was grasped within the furl of her body, where she had pulled it close for extra warmth. A second blanket lay wadded at her feet.

Les twisted around just enough to take stock of where everyone was. Jesse stood rigid and unreadable several feet behind them. Andy was on the opposite side of the enclosure moving something around.

"Katy, go see about Andy." Les ordered.

She immediately got up and noticed Andy piling wood on what had been a campfire. She went to help and by the time she gathered what was left of sticks and driftwood, a fire blazed behind her. She turned and looked at him. He was staring into the flickering blaze, his eyes brimming in silent pain. This young boy was in such turmoil. What he must have experienced tonight that no child should have.

She dropped her offering close to the fire circle and went to him to put an arm around his shoulders.

"You did a good job tonight, honey. The best anyone could do in these circumstances," she whispered against his ear. "It'll be okay. God's got this."

His shoulders shook as the hot anguish spilled over and dripped off of his chin. He heard her words and understood them, but they didn't penetrate deep enough to bring relief to his little boy soul. He knew Reeny was dead. He had been the only hope she and her baby had and he failed. Andy's heart was hurting in a way he hadn't been aware existed. He felt like curling up beside Reeny and going with her. But he just stood still and cried.

Les had sent Katy away for her own sake, before he gently took the blanket that Reeny's lifeless arms held. He knew there would be a tiny body hidden under the folds. It's umbilical cord was still attached to its mother.

Even though it had been a few years ago, Kaitlyn had given birth to their son too early and blamed her own negligence for his death. The last time she had spoken of their baby, she cried. He wanted to spare her this.

Les quickly cut the cord with his pocket knife, tied it off and gently wrapped the deceased infant girl. He believed the baby had been stillborn. Judd Luke took the bundle and held it close, willing the cold little baby to feel his love.

Les continued to search for a pulse in the mother. She had lost a lot of blood, but her color was still good. He turned her flat on her back and began CPR. That's when a second pair of hands appeared to lay on the girl's chest. Les cut his eyes up at Jesse and nodded his head.

The pair worked together for what seemed forever, before finally deciding it was useless. Les reached and took Jesse's hand over the top of the girl's body and said a prayer that she would live forever with Him.

The two men stood up, both with tears spilling over, as Judd lay his tiny bundle in the crook of Reeny's arm. No one spoke or moved. No one could.

The still silence in that place had become thick, almost like a cloud had come in and was holding them all in a frozen trance. It was a peaceful feeling. This moment belonged to the mother and child lying on the ground. They all knew it and stood respectfully reticent.

At first, Donny was surprised when he saw his beautiful young wife a short distance away, walking toward him. But then it seemed like the most natural thing to see her here. It didn't cross his mind that she had to have died to get here. She wasn't dead, but more alive and more beautiful than he remembered.

She wore a white gown similar to his, except hers was femininely gathered around her midriff and had short puffy sleeves. And her hair. He couldn't remember her long blonde strands laying in that kind of billowy light. It made him think of vanilla whipped crème. He could see without actually looking down that she was barefoot like he was. At the same time, he could see she wasn't alone. In her arms lay a tiny baby. A little white gown and the top of its head was the only part he could really see. Black hair just like his and Jesse's. And their mom's. *That's a plus.*

Yes, she fits right in, doesn't she? His mother's joy engulfed her from head to foot.

She.

You have a daughter.

He recognized that even though he and his mother were talking, they weren't speaking audibly. Communication here was more by thoughts, even though they had spoken audibly when they first saw each other. Either way seemed perfectly normal.

He hadn't had enough experience yet with speaking with his thoughts and forgot his next thought was as good as blasted on a loud speaker.

She doesn't know that baby really isn't mine—that she was conceived by...

I know all about the little girl. Everyone here knows Reeny. We've long been praying her through the hardships she had to face on the earth. You, Donny, were chosen, in our Lord's perfect time, to rescue her from her suffering.

But, why did she suffer so long? Why couldn't she be rescued before she endured so much pain?

Son, when you are able to hear that truth, you will be given the answer. For now, your obedience has blessed you with a wife who will love you with a greater love than you've known. Her child has become your own daughter, forever, by God's divine blessing.

In the next moment, Donny was facing Reeny and standing only a step away from her. A radiant smile covered her whole face when she saw him. Their eyes locked and exchanged an intimate union on the inside of each of them that far surpassed what they had suppose was love while on the earth. Love in this new realm was complete in ways that earth knows nothing about. At least, that was Donny's take on it. And it appeared to be Reenys, too. Their oneness was truly that. One-together.

When she held the infant toward him, Donny took his daughter in his arms and felt his heart warm in an emotional bonding that a daddy would naturally have for his own child. His tears dripped down onto the baby's head, seeming to mark her with a name. She was his. She was a Brandon.

Reeny closed the gap then and put her arm around her husband's waist. Instantly, his mother stood in front of them and Donny knew, somehow, what he had to do. He kissed his little girl's forehead and held her out to his mom. She would be staying with her grandmother. He knew he was leaving her in perfect and loving hands.

Jesse saw it. He *knew* he did. He watched intently, staring hard at the dead girl's right hand. Then it happened again. Her fingers moved. Two of them. That hand rested on the little bundle lying in the crook of her arm.

Jesse broke the hush in the cave when he moved to her and dropped to his knees. He grasped her hand and at that moment something broke inside of him. He wanted more than anything else at that moment for Reeny Brandon to live. He wanted her to live for Donny's sake. But he wanted her to live because he knew she had never had the chance to truly live and love and be whoever she was meant to be.

Her baby daughter would never get that chance. She never got to draw a breath, to be coddled by loving parents, to run and play or ride a horse or have a dog. Or know what it felt like to fall in love or...the joy of giving birth to a child.

Reeny never got to live normally. Probably not for one day.

Jesus, give her back her life. Give her the chance to live. Forgive me. Forgive me.

He realized the hand he was holding was warm. Not cold. He felt for a pulse. It was there.

"She's alive!"

By this time, everyone was on their knees gathered around the girl. Judd picked up the baby and handed off the blanketed bundle to Kaitlyn. The men worked quickly jerking off their coats and vests wrapping her up as warm as they could. Jesse was down to just a thin t-shirt, then grabbed the second blanket that was wadded in the dirt and ran outside to shake it out. It wrapped around her twice holding in the warmth of the rest of the clothes.

It was getting light outside now and appeared that the storm was over. Jesse picked Reeny up and headed outside. Judd went down the cliff side first and acted as a stop while Jesse slid on his butt most of the way keeping a tight hold on his young sister-in-law. Judd took over and carried her most of the way through the woods. They didn't stop at the cabin, but Jesse slid inside the front passenger seat and held the unconscious girl while Judd blew the dually down the highway on a wing and a prayer…literally a prayer.

Judd had honked his horn on the way past the house and slowed enough to yell out the window that Andy was fine and would be coming in shortly.

"Honk the boys back in, Hank, and send them on home for me," Judd yelled, then rolled the window back up.

After the men had left the cave with the girl, Les was stopped short at the sight of his wife sitting beside the fire and rocking the covered infant. He thought his heart would stop. But when he approached her, she smiled up at him.

"She should have a funeral service…With flowers and a nice marker."

Les nodded.

Andy had smothered the fire with a mound of dirt and was standing toward the back of the cave wall shivering. None of them had coats, but there were no complaints. Les sensed that Andy was keeping his distance from the baby. He took her from Kaitlyn and they made their way down the steep slope and finally back to the ranch house.

Laura, Hank and Martha were all standing in the middle of the ranch yard when the trio walked up.

"Andy!" Laura ran and grabbed him in a hug. He didn't respond other than to pull out of her grasp and walk toward the back door of the house.

"Andy?" She was confused and trying not to be hurt.

"Leave me alone, Mom."

Kaitlyn walked up and put her arm around Laura's waist. "Give him a little time. He's been through a lot. If you've got some coffee, I'll fill you in." She reached for Martha hand and pulled her alongside. "You too, Ms. Martha. We need some girl chat."

Hank had followed Les to Jesse's dually where it had been left close to the back door. Les laid his little bundle on the front passenger seat, shook hands with Hank and told him what was wrapped in the blanket.

An hour and a half later, Hank pulled Jesse's dually as close to the hospital ER doors as possible and parked. Les wanted to hold the infant as long as he could. He didn't even know the baby's name, but couldn't conceive of just laying the tiny body on the truck seat for the ride to Jackson. This little person had not lived a moment on earth, but still had managed to find a permanent home in a few big ole cowboy's hearts. She would be living with all of them from now on.

All the questions he had about this whole ordeal were yet to be answered. What in God's name had happened last night? He knew he wasn't the only one wanting answers.

Reluctantly, he handed the infant's body over to the ER doctor. They had been alerted that he was on his way with her, knowing that the young lady brought in earlier was the mother.

Law enforcement had already gotten Jesse and Judd's statements. Les was escorted from the ER into a small conference room for questioning. In the end, it was Andy they needed to complete their report. Up to this point, no one knew Andy's story, except Andy.

Jesse knew he had to rush back to the ranch for that meeting. But after being told that Donny had experienced a seizure of some kind during the night and stopped breathing for a few minutes, he suddenly felt his fatigue slam through his body. He hadn't had time to be tired, but he couldn't ignore it now. He sat down in the ICU waiting room opposite Judd and Hank. Les remained standing, but leaned against the wall. Jesse didn't care that tears trickled down his face. He laid his Stetson on the floor beside his chair and rubbed his black stubble beard roughly with both hands. He brushed unapologetically at the salty wetness.

The cup of hot coffee Hank suddenly produced seemed to revive him enough to feel like he might make it.

"Thank you. All of you."

"Think nothing of it, Jesse," Judd answered. "Any one of us would do it again in a skinny minute." The *preach* in him wanted to say more, to offer some hope with his words, but wisdom said, *let it be.*

Les finally took a seat and they sat in silence, waiting on Jesse.

In five minutes, he stood. "Reeny's alive, but critical. Donny's stable. Restland Funeral Home is coming to get the baby." He twisted his hat a couple rounds in his hands, then settled it on his head. "Let's all go home."

Jesse and Laura were the only ones allowed in the room while the police questioned Andy. He sat on the small sofa in the ranch office and recalled every detail from the time he walked to the Honeymoon cabin until he walked back to the ranch house with Les and Kaitlyn Kane and Reeny's baby.

Laura was livid, but it was mostly fear at her son's story. What he had experienced was more than most adults could have handled. And here he was, reliving the entire ordeal with his usual calm demeanor. That was the thing that was holding Laura together. His matter-of-fact, another-day-at-the-dude-ranch attitude. She realized how close her son had come to losing his life. First, his close encounter with the men who wanted to hurt an innocent young girl and then getting swept away in flood waters. And here he sat, like it was all in a day's work.

Jesse knew Andy was not as alright as he seemed. He was a real smart kid and more adult acting than some adults he'd known. He knew how to not upset his mother. But he was still a kid. And he had experienced a traumatizing event that wasn't going to let him *cool hand Luke* his way out of it. Not entirely.

"Okay, Andy. We're nearly done here, son. Investigator Cory James had been soft spoken and gentle with his questions." I need you to think real hard. Did you hear any other name other than Mr. Bender?"

After a few seconds, he shook his head. "No, sir. I don't remember any other name."

"Alright." He shook Andy's hand and thanked him before motioning Jesse to follow him outside.

He stopped beside the patrol car that was waiting. "Jesse, I've got air search on the way and there'll be a man hunt of this area on the ground. Keep your family close in. Doors locked, etc. I hope to talk to Mrs. Brandon as soon as she's able. I'll have a deputy patrolling your ranch grounds around the clock. What happened to your brother sounds like it could be tied in with the rest of this mess." They shook hands.

"Thank you, Cory."

"I'll be in touch."

Jesse had managed to work the rest of the day away. Livestock needed hay and cubes and pens needed mucked.

Andy cleaned the petting zoo pens and turned out a couple horses to run.

Laura watched her husband and son from the kitchen door while they moved around the ranch grounds as if nothing had happened the night before. But she knew they were both exhausted after more than twenty-four hours without sleep.

Never mind the trauma they'd both experienced all night long. They couldn't last much longer. Something had to give.

Hank and Martha had spent hours the past night making stew and cornbread and a chocolate cake. Enough to last a couple of days. Martha put the two little ones down for naps before she and Hank went home to rest.

"We'll be back this evening to stay the night," Martha insisted.

When Laura started to protest, Hank put up a hand.

"Now don't go spoiling our fun. You and Jesse and that boy out there needs time to yourselves. And we need them grandbabies to keep us young."

She smiled and nodded, then closed the kitchen door behind them. *Bless them, Lord.*

Les hit the light switch beside the front door. All five lamps that set around the cozy den of the foreman's log cabin went out at once. He stood there in silence for awhile letting the darkness comfort him. This was the first moment he'd had alone since cutting the cord of that little dead baby away from it's mother. It was his hands that had physically separated them—his hands that removed the tiny girl from her first love.

His compassion for the animals he cared for was strong enough to bring him to tears at times. He'd removed dead colts and calves and puppies from their bawling, begging mothers, then gone home and cried worse than they had.

But this thing he'd done today—it wanted to take him to his knees. All day he'd fought off the buildup in his chest, the burning behind his eyes. He knew Reeny Brandon had gathered the baby in her arms after giving birth. She'd wrapped it in a blanket and held the bundle in her arms. Did she know her baby was dead? Did she know she'd had a daughter?

For the first time, he understood the trauma Kaitlyn went through when she held her baby boy—his own son—just to say goodbye. Until he had removed the little girl from her mother's grip today with his own hands, he just thought he had understood Kaitlyn. Today, he knew, and he stood in the dark and let his grief for Danny roll unchecked down his cheeks.

Kaitlyn had already climbed into their king log bed at the back of the house after sharing a long hot shower. They probably hadn't missed showering together three times in their three years of marriage. Les figured the ordeal in the cave today might leave her a little subdued, but surprisingly she was holding up, true to form. He checked the door locks and headed down the hall to the bedroom by the faint nightlight in the kitchen.

Just the top of her light brown head could be seen sticking out from under a mound of quilts. It had been her idea to turn down the wintertime heat and pile on the blankets. Made sense to his cold natured birthday suit. Snuggling with that little barn queen gave new meaning and excitement to frigid winter nights. But he still didn't believe she had escaped todays experience completely unscathed.

He slid under the covers and reached to pull her into the crook of his warmth. As soon as he touched her taut muscled arm, he knew. She was crying.

"Hey."

She tried to resist, but he strong-armed her backward a couple inches and scooted himself closer until he had her bare skin spooned in against him. He threw his leg across hers and wrapped his arm snug around her. Then, she broke.

He didn't talk, but held her until she cried it out.

Daniel Les Kane, his and Kaitlyn's infant son, was buried on her family's homeplace in Missouri. The pregnancy had ended at about four months, but his wife had endured the trauma and heartache alone. They weren't married at the time and he didn't know about the baby until a couple of years later. It was his own selfish fault.

When he watched her rocking the deceased infant today in the cave, he knew the memories would reawaken.

"Les?"

"Hmm."

"I'm okay now."

He turned her over onto her back, but kept his arms around her. "I'm sorry you had to see that baby."

"It's not that. I feel so bad for the mother. I don't know if she knows her baby is gone. Maybe she's dead now, too."

"I called High Point a little bit ago. Jesse had talked to the hospital and she and Donny were both resting okay for now. One of the funeral homes has the baby."

"I just don't understand why babies have to die. They don't get to have a life. It's so unfair."

"A lot of things are unfair in this world, Katy," he said gently. "We have to pick up and move on...keep going forward."

He kissed the top of her head, then the tip of her nose. He kissed her lips softly, gently. "But, we have to take time to grieve when unfair circumstances happen. It's okay to cry."

She felt her chest begin to ache. *Doesn't he realize this is a bad time to be so tender and sympathetic?* She covered her face with her hands and turned into his broad rock-hard chest. The tightening security of his arms brought more tears.

"Everybody's asleep," Jesse sighed as he sat down on the edge of the bed and shed his socks, then sweats.

"Andy?" Laura had felt her son's demand for solitude without him saying a word. It hurt to see him struggling so hard with his emotions, but Laura went to bed early and gave him and Jesse space to sort things out.

"Andy, too."

Jesse propped up with two bed pillows behind his back and head and stuck his long legs under the cover. No matter how exhausted he was, he refused to turn out his lamp until he apologized to his wife. After what he'd witnessed up in that cave, nothing seemed so important now…nothing outside of loving his family as though his life might end today. He wasn't even sure at this moment why he thought the world would end if Donny didn't get himself a college degree. *He* didn't have one and God knew he was successful in all the right places. Just look at what was lying beside him in this once lonely bed.

And she thought his didn't stink to boot! If he had a horse whip on the place, which he didn't, he'd use it on himself.

"You should be wiped out by now," Laura said, without looking at him. "Why don't you turn your lamp off?"

He leaned his head back on his pillow and cut his eyes toward her. "Because I need to see that we are alright first."

The hurt that his words and attitude earlier had sank into her, suddenly rose up. As much as she had tried to put it to rest, his mention of it awakened it.

"Of course we're alright, Jesse. You're just tired."

"This minute, I'm tired. Earlier today, I was a self-absorbed ass." He saw the flicker of pain in her eyes. Not something he was used to seeing in his wife.

He reached out and covered her hand with his. "I'm really sorry, baby. I know that's not much of an offering after the way I treated you."

She didn't respond immediately, still needing a minute or two to let his apology settle in.

At her hesitation, he squeezed her hand. "Tell you what. Come morning, we'll sneak off to the barn before anybody wakes up and I'll lay down in the hay…or on the concrete, depending on how mad you still are, and you can stomp me to a mud hole."

Laura's sudden roar of laughter expelled the rest of the strain between them.

"So, you like that, do you?"

Her giggle box flipped over.

"Well, tired as I am, you better set the alarm. I might not wake up in time for my stompin'. Of course, you being the *stompee* and all, you'll probably wake right up and..."

Tears ran down her face as her cackles continued. "Would—you shut—up!"

Jesse burst out laughing, and then rolled over on top of her before sliding further under the quilt. "Yes, mam, I *will* shut up. Got better things to do now than not shut up!" He kissed her like it was the last chance he would ever have, just before he yanked the covers over both their heads.

***

CHAPTER SEVEN

"I have a daughter."

"That's wonderful, Mr. Brandon. I bet she'll be happy to see her dad." The ICU nurse set the controls on the I.V. and began gathering up the various tubes and other trash. "How old is she?"

"She was just born. She has lots of black hair—like mine. She's beautiful like Reeny."

The nurse stopped and stared at Donny's face a few long seconds. He was awake and seemed alert. His eyes were clear. In fact, they sparkled like two blue diamonds. For a man who had suffered such violent head trauma, he seemed a little too bright and clear.

She shoved the refuse in her hands into the trash and followed up with her latex gloves. She knew who Reeny Brandon was and the story of her stillborn baby that was brought in. Reeny was in the next ICU room.

"Mr. Brandon, how do you feel this morning?"

"Did Reeny come back?" He implored her with his eyes seeming not to have heard her question. "Did she come back?"

"Reeny is here." She pressed the nurse's station call button. When they answered, "Page Dr. Redmond ASAP to this room." She wanted to ask Donny more questions but she wasn't allowed under his circumstances. "You rest now. Your doctor will be here in a few minutes." She knew he wasn't thinking clearly, understandably, but the clarity in his face and eyes was causing her confusion. The two were usually telltale signs that coincided. Something was odd here.

In five minutes, Dr. Redmond walked in, already briefed by the nurse.

"Hey there, Donny." The doctor was smiling, but searching his patient's eyes. "I see you're back with us. Glad you're feeling better."

"Yeah, I'm not…sure what got me here."

"Tell me what you remember."

He stared off into his memory bank for a few seconds. "I was driving home from town. It was snowing." He squinted his eyes, thinking hard. "I don't remember getting home. Did I have a wreck?"

"What we know is you were found on the side of the road. You have a head injury, plus a few bumps and bruises. Your vehicle was gone."

Donny was silent awhile as he tried to remember.

"Who found me?"

"Your brother. I understand there was a dog lying on top of you. He may have kept you warm enough to have helped save your life."

"Pup. She's a she. Belongs to Jesse, but we all claim her. Or maybe she claims us."

The doctor was satisfied that Donny's thinking processes were normal.

"The nurse said my wife is here. I want to see Reeny. Let her come in here."

"Who's raising the ruckus in here?"

The doctor turned around, glad to see a family member show up right about now. "Hello, Jesse."

They shook hands and then Jesse stepped to Donny's bedside and patted him on the leg. "Looks like somebody finally decided nap time is over. How you feeling?"

"Happy slappy laying here under all these drugs. Just trying to figure out what happened to me." He looked at his brother, waiting for whatever input he had.

"We've pieced a thing or two together, but not all of it. It appears your truck was stolen right out from under you near the ranch gate. You remember how that might have happened?"

After a minute, Donny shook his head. “No. I remember driving home in the snow and next thing I know, I woke up in…” *Heaven? Oh Jesus.*

“Jesse, get Reeny. I need to talk to her.”

Jesse exchanged glances with the doc before he spread his hands on the side of the bed and leaned closer, resting his weight on one leg.

“Reeny’s here. She’s in the next room. She’s critical, Donny. They’re doing everything possible to save her life.”

Donny stared almost blankly for a long minute. He recalled his visit in Heaven. Reeny was there at the same time. The baby. She had a girl. She didn’t stay with the baby. She had to have come back…with him.

“She came back. She died, but she came back. She brought our daughter and we left her there.” He tried to rise up, the memory of that incredible event shooting his pulse rate too high.

The doctor stepped out and ordered a sedative for him.

“She won’t die again, Jesse. She came back. She came back.”

The hypo took effect within seconds and he became drowsy.

“That’s right, little brother. She’ll be fine and so will you. Get some sleep.”

Outside of the room, Jesse questioned the doctor about how much Donny was told.

"Jesse, he hasn't been conscious to be told anything until this morning. His first words to his R.N. were that he had a daughter."

Jesse stared with rounded eyes into the space in front of him. He could see Reeny's lifeless body lying on the floor of the cave. She had no pulse. He and Les worked hard to make her heart start beating. They gave up. She was dead. Then she moved her fingers. He'd seen it himself. She came back. *She won't die again, Jesse. She came back. I have a daughter.* How could Donny have known these things?

"You all right, Jesse?"

When he snapped back, the doc was staring hard at him. "Yeah, um, how's Reeny?"

He motioned for him to follow and led the way into the next room.

The respirator noise and so many various tubes in her mouth and nose made him stop in the doorway and seriously consider backing out. One thing was for sure. Doctoring wasn't in his life's calling.

He finally stepped closer to the bed. Her long blonde hair was cleaner and pulled into a knot on top of her head. Even through all of the plastic and tape around her face, he could see she was very pretty. Very young. How anyone could want to hurt this child in the way they did was beyond his understanding. He could think of a couple of real good tormenting *right back at you's* for the filth that had hurt her. He'd start with dear old dad.

"Will she survive?"

"She's improving. I feel safe in saying she'll pull through."

His eyes seemed to be locked on Reeny's face. Without moving, he asked, "What exactly happened to Donny yesterday?"

"We aren't sure. He stopped breathing for a couple of minutes. Tests didn't show anything particular. After we resuscitated him, he seemed stronger than before."

Jesse turned then and offered his hand. "Thank you for the call this morning."

"Well, sorry it came at 4am."

"Don't apologize. The time doesn't matter. Keep me informed on any changes."

Jesse didn't know what to think and decided during the drive home to set his thoughts on his son for now.

Andy was extremely resilient for his nearly twelve years, but a grown man would have a hard time knowing where to place this event in his head. Maybe that was just it. Children can lay things like that aside, especially with a real simple explanation from their parent. Andy was one to take on an adult role the best he could and then ponder the end results a little too seriously. He was just old enough now to let his thoughts and *coulda, shoulda's* get him into trouble.

He pulled up and parked his dually in front of the barn. Andy was sitting on the aspen log that lay along the outside wall of the barn. Pup lay on her back in the warm sun at Andy's feet, enjoying a belly rub from her young master. She seemed to have come through her ordeal easily enough.

He clicked the truck door shut and walked over and squatted beside Pup. Andy sat up straight while Jesse took a turn at the belly rub.

"Nice to see the sun shining for a change."

"Yes, sir." Andy attempted a grin, but didn't look up.

Jesse noticed Rebel Man, his stallion, prancing on the hot walker behind the barn. "I assume you put Rebel out?"

He nodded.

"I appreciate that. I haven't had time to take care of him."

Andy wouldn't look up. He was too quiet—too distant.

"I want to ask you a question, son, and I want you to be honest with me."

He nodded, still occupied with Pup.

"Are you thinking you're responsible in some way for what happened in that cave yesterday?"

Andy stopped petting the dog and stared blankly at the ground a minute.

"I shouldn't have left her. I should have kept the fire going."

Jesse shook his head. "No, Andy. That little baby was gone to Heaven before she got all the way born. You couldn't have saved her. She was just born too soon. Reeny is getting better. The doctor thinks she'll be alright."

Andy stood up. "I was about to put Rebel Man up."

When he hurried off at a fast walk, Jesse knew the answer to his question. His son was understandably in a lot of turmoil.

He made a round through the barn, looking in every occupied stall. Andy had taken care of the feed and water for the horses. The petting zoo chores were done as well. He took a deep breath and decided to give Andy his space a while longer.

He took off his hat and lowered his face. *Lord God, my boy needs some help. I'd appreciate it if You'd show us the way to get through this. Thank You.* He replaced his hat and went to the house.

Andy let out his breath standing alone in the alleyway of the barn. His dad had left and he didn't know if he felt abandoned or relieved. He didn't feel like talking about what happened and he didn't want to be around everybody right now either. Alone felt scary. Maybe he'd take a walk with Pup. He never felt alone with her and she made his insides feel more comfortable.

"Come on, girl."

Obediently she was on her feet, tail wagging. The pair set out toward the creek where a swimming hole had been roped off for summertime dudes. He had spent a lot of time there, he and Pup, the past couple of years. Jesse had taught him to swim when he was five, but he'd taken lessons in Jackson to earn a lifeguard certificate in order to help monitor the ranch guest swimmers. He had his own lifeguard watch-tower on the creek bank, compliments of his mom and dad for earning his certification.

In fact, anything he ever wanted to learn, his parents simply said, go for it. Then they got whatever he needed to help him accomplish it.

When he was six, Uncle Donny had seen him mostly destroying a good lariat, trying to rope a set of dummy steer horns. He told him—*if you're going to do it, do it right.* Roping lessons started that day and when he was ten, his parents gave him his own seasoned roping horse. He had already cut a few roping teeth working with the cowboys at the Double OO. He could throw a rope now almost as good as any hired cowhand.

And driving—Jesse let him learn to drive when he was eight, as long as he stayed off the road. But once, before he was nine, he drove the five highway miles to the Double OO in the old ranch pickup to find his dad. His mom was lying in the kitchen floor, over due to have his baby brother and she couldn't get up. She had been really mad when she heard what he'd done. His dad shook hands with him and said, *good job, kid, but don't let it happen again.* That memory made him smile.

And Dr. Les Kane gave him some hands on experience stitching up a baby calf's cut leg.

And he, more than anything, wanted to learn how to shoot a rifle. His dad set up for target practice and taught him to shoot straight and accurate.

All of this attention and he was having his twelfth birthday in a few weeks. A boy couldn't ask for more opportunities to be laid in his lap than what he'd had. He was well aware that he had a good life…a great life.

But right now, he felt like a total failure—like he could hardly stand to be alive. A baby died because of him. That was Uncle Donny's little baby. He should have done something different. He sort of knew what to do. He could have been there when the baby came out and done what Dr. Les had done, even though he got there too late. Andy had watched animals giving birth and a lady giving birth when he watched a sex education program on the computer. He watched what to do, but he panicked. Reeny will hate him now. And Uncle Donny, too.

He walked toward the canyons that were just below Gramps and Granny Martha's cabin. He'd been there before. Those canyons felt lonely and sometimes, scary. And that's how he felt today—lonely and scared. He didn't want to be alone. He didn't want company either. Confusion was twisting up his insides.

Toni Luke watched her husband pace nervously across the backyard and back to the patio lounge chair where she was sitting. His spurs jangled while bits of alfalfa hay jarred from the creases in his jeans and dusty blue chambray shirt. His two-day growth of beard didn't cover the smudges of dust and probably cow poop. With Judd, you never knew. He was all cowboy at heart and was neck deep in the ranch work along with his hands most days. Toni was generally of a mind to work alongside him, but at this stage of her pregnancy, Judd refused to let her near the barn.

Abigail Luke was nine years old now and finally getting her biggest wish granted. A baby sister.

Toni didn't ask Judd what was wrong. She had watched this happen to him many times. His relationship with Almighty

God was one that defied reasoning and she didn't even try. Many nights, usually after midnight in the wee hours, she would find him on his knees or lying prostrate on the floor praying to the Lord. And many times, like this one, the Spirit of God would move him to do something particular or drop what he was doing and pray. Or someone would suddenly show up needing to talk or to be prayed for. He never knew what it was until it happened.

He was obviously pacing with the power of God on him for a job He needed him to do. Toni just stayed still, but prayed for her husband to hear clearly whatever it was.

Judd had received a commission from the Lord to preach right out of their home several years ago. He simply called it Cowboy Church Meeting. Sunday services had grown to such now that they'd talked about moving it to the barn. Cowboys and their families from neighboring ranches attended and now there were several coming out from Jackson Hole. Cowboy Church was Judd's first priority and today he'd dropped everything to watch and pray for whatever his mission was.

He was standing with his face up to the sun, eyes closed, when the unrest in his soul settled. It eased away just like it had come—unexpectedly. Judd looked across the field toward the west, waiting to be sure of what was moving through his mind. It seemed strange, but the compelling was constant.

He jangled back over to where his beautiful and very pregnant *bride* was sitting. He had referred to her as that since their wedding a decade ago. He leaned down and kissed her lips.

“I have to go somewhere. Not far. Over by the Walton’s place. I’d tell you more, but I don’t know more.”

She smiled. “I get that. Be careful.”

He left and headed toward the canyon area where Kaitlyn Kane had gotten lost several years ago. He just hoped his mind wasn’t playing tricks. Seemed to him that this type of thing should be so black or white that there would never be room for doubts to plague him. But he always had to battle through. *Is God talking to me or did my mind slip a gear?* Either way, he had reasoned with himself a long time ago. It was better to follow through with what he believed his Heavenly Father was saying than chance failing Him. His goal as God’s preacher for this small area was to always be listening for Him. That had become second nature after years of practice. It had also become an exciting and joyful existence, but a primal need—necessary to sustain his life.

There was only one person who could truly understand his friendship with the unseen God. That was Donny Brandon. Others respected his deep love for God. And still others ridiculed him for it.

He reached up and pulled the sun visor down. The highway wound back to the east for a short distance. The sun was as bright as he’d ever seen it.

He recalled then another bright light he’d seen once. Brighter than the sun bouncing off of his windshield. This light wasn’t blinding, but seemed to envelope his whole being.

He’d been an angry young boy that grew into an angry man. His parents hadn’t measured up to his *perfect* expectations of them and everybody after that was suspect and held at arm's length.

Standing in the bathroom of his boyhood home, after threatening his pregnant wife with horrendous abuse, the filth of his own angry soul overwhelmed him until he'd dropped to his knees in repentance and surrender to Jesus Christ. When he'd finally been able to stand to his feet, the room was filled with a strange kind of Light—A beautiful, peaceful brilliance. That was the moment he'd started to become a real man—To his family—To his God.

The one thing he would never let himself do was forget the ugliness of his own failures, because he never wanted to make the mistake of judging another's mistakes.

Having no idea what he was supposed to be looking for, he drove slowly and listened more than looked. He was strictly on God's time and purpose, following, literally, by blind faith. His mind wanted to tell him he was insane even driving out here. But he believed God and simple trust was moving him to drive on.

The red rock canyons came into view as he came up over a rise just before he would reach the Walton's cabin. With no clue what he was looking for, he scanned the highway out in front of his vehicle and then the rock walls and valleys off to his left.

He had half way expected this to turn out to be more his imagination than a God-trip. That had happened before.

Then he saw the dog. He pulled off to the side of the road as far as possible, parked and got out. That was Jesse's old dog, alright. She sat on her haunches staring down into a gully that Judd couldn't see from where he was. He didn't know if old Pup usually strayed off this far or not, but he'd better check on her. He crossed the barbed wire fence and headed to a spot that looked the easiest to navigate downward. The trail was muddy and slick. He stopped half way down and called to her.

"Pup! Hey girl...Come here."

She turned her head and studied him, ears alert. Her tail began to pop up and down on the rock she sat on when she recognized him, but didn't get up.

Finally when he made his way to her, she got up and whined, twisting her body back and forth in welcome.

"Hey, young lady. What on earth are...?"

Then he saw Andy. He was sitting cross-legged on the muddy red ground about six feet down, his hands covering his face. Pup was standing guard and Andy didn't act like he knew he had company. Judd could hear him crying. He didn't want to intrude, but he knew God had sent him out here. No doubts now. He rubbed and patted Pup's face and head before carefully sliding down the embankment to where Andy sat. He squatted beside the boy and spoke without touching him.

"You sure know where all the good hide-outs are. Guess that comes with being a real good explorer."

He didn't respond.

"Do you mind having some company? Maybe, talk a little?"

Andy swiped his palms across his face, but didn't look up or answer.

"I'm going to level with you, son, because you're smart enough and mature enough for me to do that. I didn't find you here by accident. Almighty God put into me to drive out this way. He knew you were here and needed some help with this thing. What happened in that cave was tragic—A hard thing to have to experience." He paused a few seconds. "I'll just sit here until you're ready to talk."

Judd twisted around to look up at Pup. She was lying down, but her ears were perked up like a sentry on guard.

Finally, after about five minutes, Andy rested his forearms on his crossed knees and turned his face partly toward Judd.

"I left Reeny by herself. I was trying to get help, but the flood trapped me. I should have tried to swim out of the brush pile. But…I got scared. I couldn't turn loose of the tree limbs." Fresh tears began to flow.

"And you believe you're responsible for what happened to Ms. Reeny and her baby because you couldn't get help soon enough?"

He nodded, his face crinkling with barely controlled sobs.

Holy Spirit of God, give me the right words to help this boy.

After a minute, "Andy, everything that happened was beyond your control. If anything, you're a hero in all this. That little baby was stillborn. She was already in Heaven before her body entered this world. And…Andy, look at me."

He cut his puffy eyes up at Judd.

"In a situation like this, life and death is God's call. Not ours. If He'd intended for that little girl to grow up on this earth, He'd have left her here."

"But that's just it. She didn't get to grow up."

"That's not true, Andy. She won't grow up here on the earth, but she'll grow up in Heaven. She's very much alive."

His expression went from extreme emotional despair to wide eyes full of surprise. "But, how…how…"

"Let me explain it this way. There's three parts to the human being. We are spirit, soul and body. Three parts. God made us in His own image. So we are all spirit beings like He is a Spirit being. But to live on the earth, we need a human body for our spirits to live inside of." He held up his arm and pinched his skin. "That's this flesh and bone right here. And the soul is simply our mind. What we think and reason and feel emotion with."

Andy was glued to Judd's face as he explained, soaking up every word like a sponge.

"So when that little baby girl stopped living, even inside of her mother's body, she had no use for the flesh and bone body. Her little spirit rose up out of her body and she was taken to Heaven to live."

Judd could see questions sparking like fireworks in his big browns.

"*Who* took her to Heaven?"

"Angels, probably."

"So, are angels the people who have already died?"

"No. We don't become angels. You'll always be Andy Parker, even in Heaven. Angels are spirit beings created just to be angels. They're God's helpers."

"Do you think Uncle Donny and Reeny know about that. About their baby being alive and all."

"I'm sure we'll get the chance to talk to them and find out. I hear they are both doing much better."

Andy nodded.

Seeing a frown suddenly coat his face, Judd knew there was more. He waited.

"Mr. Luke, have you ever felt like you *have* to do something, but knowing at the same time you were doing something wrong."

He thought for a minute. "Possibly. Why don't you explain what you mean."

"Well, I've been going up to the cave for a while. I found it by accident one day and I took camping stuff up there, but I never camped. Then I gathered up firewood. It was summertime, but I couldn't quit hauling loads of firewood up there. Then I just stopped and left everything there. I didn't go back until that night with Reeny."

Listening to his story sent chills up and down Judd's spine. He could clearly see the set-up.

"Why do you think you were doing something wrong?"

"Because I was way outside the boundary of where I could go exploring. I knew I wasn't supposed to go that far, but I couldn't stop."

Judd was speechless for a few minutes. All he could think at the moment was *what an awesome God he served!* He knew this kid had no idea how God had used him in advance of a coming tragedy. He truly had been used to save Ms. Reeny Brandon's life.

He scooted his wet and muddy rear-end to a more comfortable position. "There's two things going on here. First, as you already know, your obedience to your parents is priority. God Himself put you under their authority until you reach—what is it—twenty-five?"

Andy reached over and popped him on the arm.

Judd grabbed the arm like he was pained. "Okay, okay. Eighteen, then. And with that said, the right thing would have been to tell them what you felt and get permission to go there."

"What if they said no?"

"Well, that leads to the second thing. I think you may have been led of God to stock that cave. He knew this incident was going to happen. What you did saved Reeny's life, Andy. God would have given over a little Favor with mom and dad on this deal in order to get done what He needed done. Go talk to them first chance and explain what happened. I promise you they will understand."

"I will."

Judd could see a terrible burden had lifted off of the young man. "How about I give you and your sidekick a lift home?"

He dropped the pair off at the barn and drove home, feeling like he'd just won the lottery. These God-jobs he gets to do always leave him happy and praising God. At least the ones that end like this.

“Mister Brandon, I swear! That little wife of yores ain’t gonna get no rest if you don’t quit hauntin this room! Next thang, you’ll be piled up in the bed with her.”

Donny grinned at the overweight grey headed lady wearing a nurses-aide I.D. on her blue flowery uniform.

“Now there’s a good idea. Thanks.”

“Oh no you don’t, Miz Brandon. You just holler for Masie if he gets too frisky in here. I’ll lock his scrawny butt in his own room cross the hall.”

“Now, no call to get all bent out of shape, Ms. Masie. We’re legal, you know. Not to mention, I was discharged early this morning.” He winked at his wife who was lying slightly elevated on her hospital bed.

“Yeah, well, you heard me,” she shot as she left the room.

Reeny tried to smile, but her heart was too heavy to get there. Her mind was consumed with images and pieces of memories of too many things.

Donny moved to her bedside and wrapped his arms around her. When he kissed her fully on the lips, she finally looked at him. She searched his eyes as though trying to see past them—Deep into his ocean blue soul.

“Thorn,” she whispered. “I want to see my baby. I need to see her. Where is her body?”

He sat on the edge of the bed and raked his fingers through her hair, pulling a few loose strands off of her face. “Her funeral is tomorrow, sweetheart. Jesse and a couple neighboring families arranged for a graveside service. The doctor didn’t think you’d be strong enough to go.”

"Where is she now?"

"At the funeral home."

She sat up and drew her legs underneath herself. She didn't let on that the room spun a couple of circles.

"Thorn," she grasped the front of his t-shirt, "take me to see her. I never saw her and I need to. She's my baby. Please."

Confusion struck him. Did she not remember? Maybe she wasn't actually there like he was. It was *his* dream—Or vision—Or visit to Heaven? Every detail was so clear and real.

The pleading in her eyes was too much. This was too important, too personal to tell her no. Jesse had detailed the whole story to him last night that had happened to her in the cave. He'd cried in his brothers arms for the second time in his life. After what Reeny suffered through, he knew neither hell nor fifteen hospital security guards would stop him from taking her to see her baby.

He grasped her hand that clutched at him. "Okay, angel. I'll take you there."

He glanced at the I.V. stuck in the back of her other hand. "I'll be right back." Then he rushed out of the room.

It was at least twenty minutes before he came back rolling a wheel chair. Her doctor and nurse followed him in.

"Ms. Brandon, I'm allowing this because of the unusual circumstances, but I want you back in here today. You need a few more days with me. Comprende?"

She nodded.

"I'll bring her back, doc."

Donny had called the funeral home to have them get ready for a viewing. He hadn't seen the baby yet either, but Jesse said the women had bought her a tiny lacy white gown and silk booties.

He easily carried Reeny inside, a long white robe covering her hospital gown. A tiny little pink box set on an oblong table inside of a private room. It was open and Donny set Reeny on her feet a couple steps away. He wrapped an arm tightly around her and together they took the two steps forward.

Neither of them became overly emotional. They touched her satin gown and full head of black hair and smiled at her beautiful perfection.

"We have to name her." Donny whispered against her hair.

"Her name is Bonnie."

He sucked a surprised breath. "When…did you name her that?"

"I didn't. You did. You said Bonnie means *pretty.*"

It took a few seconds for Donny to catch a good breath. She *was* there. She knew.

***

CHAPTER EIGHT

"Andy?" Reeny walked into the dim lighted barn where Laura told her she could find Andy tending to his young lambs. She could see him hunched over just inside the door of a stall along the far wall.

He stood up with a very small fuzzy ball of black fur in his arms. He turned toward her, but didn't say anything.

Reeny was aware of how the incident in the cave had affected him and wanted to help him. She had been released from the hospital two weeks ago and had to threaten her over-protective husband with bodily injury if he didn't let her out of the cabin. Of course, he roared with laughter while he escorted her over for a visit with Laura and the kids. While Thorn was engaged in a wrestling match with Anna Leigh and Jesse, Jr., she slipped out to the barn.

"Hi, Andy. What have you got there?"

"It's one of my youngest lambs. This one is the runt out of triplets."

She reached to rub its head. "Can I hold it?"

"Sure." He put the lamb in her arms and grabbed a second one and pulled it backwards before it escaped.

Reeny rubbed her face against the soft fuzz, then reluctantly handed it back. Andy headed it back toward it's mother and slid the door shut.

"I was looking for you, Andy, because I never got a chance to say thank you for what you did for me. You saved my life."

He looked down, not sure what to say.

"You were so brave. If you hadn't followed me and got me in the cave, I would have died."

He jerked his eyes up at her then. She could read his thoughts as if he'd said it out loud.

"Little Bonnie was taken to Heaven before anything could ever hurt her, Andy. She's real happy up there with her grandmother. It's really a beautiful place where she is."

"How do you know that for sure about her grandmother?"

Reeny looked unsure how to answer, then simply said, "I dreamed about it. I saw her in a dream. She was so happy."

When Andy smiled, his eyes twinkled and she put her arms around his shoulders and gave him a quick hug before heading back out into the late afternoon sun.

In reality, she didn't dream that at all. She couldn't tell Andy it was real. That she had actually visited Heaven—that she had carried her tiny newborn girl there herself. She hadn't been able to approach the subject with Thorn either. He was there too, at least, *she* knew he was. She just didn't know if *he* knew, or remembered. She was afraid he would think her brain had been damaged when she stopped breathing in the cave. He had even given Bonnie her name. *Her name is Bonnie Brandon. It means pretty.* That's what he'd said when he kissed the baby and handed her to his mother. Strangely, it didn't seem to be news to Reeny. It seemed that she already knew her daughter's name before Thorn said it.

"Hey, babe, can I give you a lift somewhere?"

Before she could answer, two strong, blue plaid shirted arms encircled her from behind. She melted into her husband's bear hug, letting her head loll back against his chest. His black beard stubble was rough against her cheek, his Stetson bumping against her hair.

"I was hoping I might run into a good looking cowboy to make my day."

"I can make your night, too, little missy. Just step into that trusty old farm pick-em-up and we'll head over to a little hide-out I know about."

She was beginning to feel tired and turned in Thorn's arms to look at his familiar and gorgeous face. His full lips smiled down at her as he dropped a warm lingering kiss on her eager mouth. But the smile didn't reach his eyes. In fact, his eyes were pained.

"Thorn?"

He pursed his lips and patted her shoulders. "Okay, let's go home first."

Neither said another word until they were inside their cabin. Reeny turned on the lamp light, while Thorn put a small flicker in the fireplace. Before stopping he put a couple cups of coffee on to drip.

When his eyes connected with hers, she was standing beside the bed, her hands folded in front of her, waiting. She was always like that—quiet, patient, waiting her turn for attention. Without looking away, he walked over and rubbed his hands up and down her upper arms, then kissed the top of her beautiful blonde head.

"Honey, Jesse got word today from the sheriff. They've discovered that your father passed away."

She didn't respond.

"Harvey Carr was found the same night you graduated. He was shot."

She stood still and silent for several minutes. She couldn't seem to feel anything. No hurt. No sympathy.

"Do they know who killed him?"

"It was ruled a suicide."

She closed her eyes a moment. *Did nobody question what happened to Reeny Carr?* That sounded so sad. She suddenly felt a pang of sorrow. Not for herself, but him. There was no place to hope for his wretched soul. He left no chance to be sorry for what he'd done. Suicide was so sad. More final sounding than other kinds of deaths.

"I feel very sorry for him," she whispered. "He can't say he's sorry for what he did to me."

"Maybe he did. Maybe he repented to God."

She nodded and accepted Thorn's warm embrace. He held her for a long time, whispering over and over in her ear what a beautiful, worthy and desirable woman she was. He always seemed to know just what she needed to hear.

He guided her to the red leather loveseat in front of the fireplace. "Get comfortable while I get our coffee."

She sat down and watched him in the kitchen. She looked at his handsome full form, standing with his back to her. He was making and serving her coffee. He loved her and she didn't know why. She didn't know what to do to keep that from changing. Love seemed to flow from the people here. They loved each other—Jesse and Laura. And they loved their children. They played and laughed with them and spoke so kind to them. Mr. and Mrs. Luke came to the hospital to see her. They hugged her and prayed for her. And Les and Kaitlyn Kane from the Luke's ranch had visited her. They'd all treated her with such love and acceptance. But the ones who loomed largest in her mind was the grandparents—The Brandon kid's grandparents, Mr. Hank and Granny Martha. She wasn't clear on whose side of the family they were from, but those dear old people sat with her at the hospital while Thorn attended their baby's funeral.

Granny Martha told her stories about the time she and Laura had re-arranged the whole dude ranch while Jesse was gone on a trip. Mr. Hank had laughed as if he'd never heard about it before.

But it was the way he had looked at his wife while they stood on either side of her bed, eyes twinkling like little round stars, both of them making her feel as though she belonged to them somehow.

Jesse had done a 360 toward her and Thorn. He couldn't be more helpful or kinder if he tried.

This place was like a little country Heaven to Reeny, set apart from all of the most unimaginable cruelties this world had to offer. What did she do to deserve being in this place with Thorn Brandon who truly loved her. *Her.*

He handed her a smoking mug and sat beside her. She noticed the concern still etched in his eyes, even though he tried to grin it away.

"Something is still bothering you."

"You don't miss much, do you?" He squeezed her knee, then slurped at the hot liquid. "Yep, there's more. For one, my dually was recovered sitting on the bottom of the river. There was a body in it."

She turned widened eyes on him. Her mind jumped from Hasi? Sir? Had to be one of them. "Who was it?"

"He didn't have any ID on him, but they told Jesse he was a small man of foreign decent. Reeny, they want…"

"Hasi."

He studied her. "Did you see him that night at the cabin?"

She shook her head. "No. He was always around with Sir. It had to be him." She stopped herself from revealing that Andy had seen two men in Thorn's dually that night. She wanted that child kept out of this now. "I told the police everything I knew when they came to the hospital—the only names I know for them."

"I know, baby. You did a good job with that considering your circumstances. But…"

"But?"

"They want you to go down and try to identify the body. I told Jesse you weren't up…"

"When?"

Donny jerked his head back, startled at the strength in her face and voice. "To—morrow."

She looked him straight in the eye. "I'll be fine, Thorn. I'll go tomorrow."

He couldn't move his eyes from hers for a minute. He hadn't seen this determined intensity on her before. Finally he nodded his head, took her empty coffee cup out of her hand and set it on the small log bench table beside his cup. He leaned over toward her, one arm stretched along the top of the seat behind her head. His other hand caressed the side of her face. "You never cease to amaze me, you know that?"

The gravelly whisper breezed hot against her face, his touch sending her pulse into overdrive. Her heart began to pound until she felt like an earthquake was travelling through her whole body. She loved the way Thorn could make her feel without any help from her. It just whammed right through her. It made her a little giddy and crazy—like she wanted to throw off all of her clothes and feel his body wrapped around hers until he completely consumed her. Where was this coming from? She'd never *ever* felt such things—never when…when…"Oh!"

She slapped her hand over her mouth and choked on the sudden disgust that swallowed up her excitement at being in her husband's arms. She pushed him backward and scrambled to her feet. Revulsion consumed her just as fast as her hammering heartbeat for Thorn's touch had done. The memory of her body being abused would not let her get closer to the man she loved.

She raced for the bathroom in the back of the cabin, but he caught her before she could shut the door.

"Hold on, Reeny." He grabbed her arm.

"Let go. I can't do this."

"Do what, baby?" He held her by her upper arms and stepped into the bathroom with her. He knew *what.* He'd already prepared himself for this possibility. She had been severely traumatized and he figured they might have a long row to hoe until she could be comfortable with him. She desperately needed him and he fully intended to see it through.

"I'm not going to touch you, Reeny. I've already told you that. I will never force sex on you. Ever."

"I know that. I *do* know that. But, I *want* to be with you Thorn. I want us to make love and be together...all the way. I feel so excited when you touch me. I *want* that, but something won't let me forget. And I think about *him* and then I feel so dirty and…" She dissolved into tears, but stayed a step back from the security of his arms.

He let her go and watched her crying into her hands. She was so young and needed a lot of emotional help. Right now he felt years older than her, but wasn't sure he would be able to give her what she needed.

"Reeny, why don't you get yourself a hot shower and dress for bed? Fact is, you're in no condition to be worrying over anything right now. You need a few weeks to get all healed up. You just need time. All the time you want."

He left her and went back into the main living area. When he heard the water come on in the shower, he took care of the coffee cups and then turned down the quilts and comforter on the bed. He left one small lamp glowing in the kitchen and along with the light from the gas fire logs, he created a soft and gentle atmosphere for his child-like bride—his bruised, tormented and *spunky* little bride.

Jesus, help me to help her.

He was sitting on the loveseat when she came back. One of the long white terry robes provided by the ranch was wrapped tightly around her, the sash tied at the waist. He couldn't stop the twinkle of approval from landing on her, but he tossed it down as quick as possible. He could tell she was attempting to cover up—her way of keeping him at arm's length. But a pair of old men's coveralls couldn't conceal her sexy self! Not from him.

After he showered, he reappeared in his black sweat pants and a short sleeve white T. Not his favorite for bed wear, but he knew Reeny needed every form of security he could provide.

She was propped in bed with pillows behind her back and had positioned his pillows the same for him. He climbed in, relishing the cushy comfort and waited. Something was working her thoughts to death. He could feel it. She was staring hard at the small flicker of fire, but he knew she wasn't seeing it. He waited.

Finally, "How did we both know our baby's name?" Her eyes never left the fire flame.

There it was. He had wanted to ask her questions about that event, too. There didn't ever seem to be a right time, til now.

He cut his eyes toward her. "What do you remember about that, Reeny?"

She lowered her eyes to stare at the bed comforter covering her legs. It was a long minute before she spoke. "I'm not sure you would understand…what…happened to me."

"If it helps, something strange happened to me, too. Maybe it's time we both talk about it."

"I'm not sure how to tell you what happened—what it *seems* like happened."

He shifted his body to his side to face her direction. "Start at the beginning. What's the first thing you can remember about…about something strange happening."

She looked off into the space of the room letting herself go back to that memory. "I remember being so cold and the pain was the worst I've ever known. I knew the baby had been born.

I couldn't hear it make any noise. It was too dark. I couldn't see, so I reached down under my bottom and felt the baby. She was cold, too and I pulled her up to my stomach and tried to get her warm…in my arms." She paused a moment. "I think I must have fallen asleep then. When I woke up, I felt stronger and warm. The baby was squirming and warm too. There was a light in the cave. It was kind of foggy, but so warm. I stood up. There was no more pain and I held the baby in my arms. But she was wrapped in a soft, white wrap. Immediately I felt something drawing me through the fog. I wasn't afraid. It felt…nice. I wanted to go wherever something was taking me. I felt safe."

Donny's breathing became shallow as he hung on to every word she said. She was actually telling him about her death in the cave. He felt the hair on his arms stand straight up.

"I guess the next thing I knew about was the flower garden." She hesitated.

"The flower garden?"

She nodded. "I found myself suddenly standing in this place—the most beautiful garden of all kinds of flowers, all colors and shapes. The smell of those flowers was like a…a perfume of some kind. I couldn't get enough of their fragrance. Even the baby was smiling. I sat down on a stone bench that set beside a path. The same kind of stone made a walking path through the flowers. But I felt I should wait there on the bench seat. That's when the lady came. She was so nice and brought me some juice to drink. I don't know what kind it was, but it tasted so good…sweet."

She frowned, squinting her eyes in deeper thought before she continued.

"I know the lady sat beside me and told me things. It seems like she talked to me a long time, but, I can't remember anything she said now. I just remember her leaving me there. Then I got up and walked down the stone path for a while."

She turned her head and looked at Thorn for the first time. "You were there where I walked to, and the lady was there with you." She searched his frozen face for some kind of recognition. "Thorn, were you really there too, or was I dreaming you…or what?"

Finally when he could make his mouth work, he nodded his head, starring her in the eyes. The most he could get out was a whisper. "I was there, Reeny."

After a stunned silence, "How? What happened to us, Thorn?"

He pushed himself up to a straighter sitting position. "I think we had what's called a Near Death Experience."

"I don't know what that is."

"Jesse told me you weren't breathing when they found you. The baby had been born and wasn't breathing either. He and Les Kane did CPR on you, but they thought you had died. But then, you suddenly started to breathe again. The baby never did."

0 "So while I wasn't breathing, I went to Heaven for a while?"

He nodded.

"But what happened to you? Did you stop breathing too?"

"They said I had some kind of seizure and quit breathing. It must have happened to both of us at the same time."

They looked at each other for a long moment, expressions ranging from stunned, to fear, to amazed.

"When you handed me…our daughter, I knew her name. It seemed like I already knew her."

"You kissed her head and said *goodbye, Bonnie*. When I was in the flower garden talking to the beautiful lady, I told her the baby was *my pretty little girl.* And, I remember she said, *little Bonnie. Bonnie means pretty*. Oh… Thorn."

He slowly got up and went to the mantel for his wallet. It took him a minute to find what he needed. Slowly he turned around with a small piece of paper in his hand, and then went around to Reeny's side of the bed. He held the paper up for her to see.

She gasped and slapped her hand to her mouth. Then she reached out and touched the photograph with her finger. "That's her! That's the lady in the flower garden. The same one you handed Bonnie to." She looked at Thorn, tears filling her eyes. Seeing the lady's face brought a sudden surge of grief—of longing for her baby. She felt an ache in her empty arms. She hadn't truly allowed herself to grieve for the greatest loss she had ever experienced. Her mouth trembled as tears spilled over.

"Who is she?"

"My mother. She died when I was twelve. Bonnie's grandmother."

"But…she's *not* her grandmother. She's not—"

"God chose me to be your baby's dad. I don't know what He did, Reeny, but something unique happened—a bonding between me and her when I held her. I felt like she was really my daughter. I think the baby felt it too. I can't explain it. But she is with her…her God-given grandmother in Heaven. I hope you don't mind that God made her a Brandon. She has a real family, here and in Heaven."

"Mind?" She tried with everything she had to stop crying, but couldn't. Too much for too long and it all wanted to gather up and wash out at once. She was so proud of the fact that her baby was accepted as a Brandon, but more than anything else, she was feeling the loss of her first born.

He moved her over and slid in beside her, then pulled her close and wrapped both arms tightly around her.

"I know I shouldn't cry. Not after what happened—but—I miss her."

Her sobs tore at his heart, but he knew she had a lot of pain to get rid of.

"No, angel girl, you *should* cry." He planted a long kiss on her forehead. "You'll always miss our Bonnie. So will I. But we got a gift, an unusual blessing that we both can remember and know *exactly* where she is."

"Why do you think this happened? Us going to Heaven together like that? I mean, what are we supposed to do with this now?"

He was silent for a while.

"I believe these kind of supernatural things belong to God, exclusively. He had to have orchestrated that whole thing. And

I also believe He has a purpose for everything He does. We need to ask Him our questions. I'm pretty sure He's the only One who would have the answers to this one."

Reeny's tears stopped. A strange hush fell over her while listening to Thorn and she relaxed and enjoyed the sweetness of it. It just dawned on her that she knew what it was like to die. And so did her husband. The easiest thing she had ever done was step out of this life on earth and into the next one in Heaven. She knew, too, that no matter what, everything was as it should be.

Slowly, she reached her arm around his middle. She massaged her open hand up and down his back and felt his arms clench tighter around her. Nothing that she could think of could ever compare to the rightness of how this felt.

***

CHAPTER NINE

The sun wasn't up yet and Jesse had no idea what time it was. Laura had thrown a towel over the digital clock beside the bed to black out the greenish light it cast over the bedroom.

But regardless, he had to get up. This was the second night in a row he'd had the same dream. He didn't want to give it a chance to pick up where it had just left off.

As quiet as possible, he slipped out of bed and made his way to the kitchen. Moonlight glimmered through the kitchen window lighting his way. He drew a glass of water and sat on a stool at the center island. A quick glance at the clock on the stove told him this was pointless. It was only a few minutes after midnight. He *had* to go back to bed.

But he *had* to figure out this dream that was haunting his deeply buried memories. He allowed himself to entertain the dream now that he was wide awake. There was no brushing it off like he did yesterday. He felt sure it would just come back again.

He downed half a glass of water, and then remembered every detail.

In the dream, he was a grown man, but sitting in an elementary school desk when in walks his dad carrying a long stemmed rose. A red rose. He walked up to Jesse where he sat and broke a long thorn off of the stem and stabbed him in the top of his head. Then he walked back out, taking the rose with him, but leaving the thorn buried in Jesse's head.

Both times, the dream had been so real that he woke up suddenly and felt the top of his head. But just now, sitting in the dark kitchen, tormented by this dream of his dad, he remembered Donny. Donny *Thorn.* Was there a connection to his brother calling himself by the hated name of Thorn and this dream? The dream didn't *have* to mean one single thing. Most are rambling bits and pieces of regurgitated two-day old pizza anyway.

He shook his head and finished his water. But not this one. He had never forgotten the words his dad spoke the very night their mom came home from the hospital carrying their newborn son in her frail, weak arms. Jesse had rushed up to peek at his new baby brother when he heard...*Thorn! He's nothin' but a thorn in my side!* Jesse didn't know until years later when he saw a copy of Donny's birth certificate for school that his name was Donny Thorn, compliments of their dad. Legally he couldn't change it, but he'd angrily made it clear to his mom and little brother that *Thorn* was never to be used or spoken. And it never was until now. Why now?

Jesse slung the cover off and sat up on the side of the bed. He reached to his bedside table and jerked the hand towel off of the lighted clock. Three a.m. He threw the towel back in place and rubbed his sleep deprived eyes. This made three times in a row for that ridiculous dream—twice just tonight!

"Jesse, honey, is something wrong?" Laura rose up and put her hand on his lower back.

"No. Everything's fine."

He didn't sound fine to her. "What time is it?"

"Three. Go back to sleep. I've got to go out to the barn."

He got up and grabbed his jeans and shirt he'd laid out for the day and went to the kitchen to put them on. He slapped his Stetson on his head, but pulled on socks, boots and coat outside the back door. No need to have kids awake at this hour.

Jesse walked with determination through the cold blustery wind to the barn. The dim nightlight he left on gave enough light for him to make his way to an empty stall down the far isle. He'd spent more time in this coveted little space than anywhere else on the ranch with the exception of his cozy, warm nest beside his wife every night. But, right now, everything and everybody was overruled by his need to talk to his Father. He needed an answer. Beyond a shadow of a doubt, he knew that he'd had a God-dream and he knew there was no one except God who could interpret it for him.

The barn was not exactly quiet, but Rebel whinnied *hello* inciting a response from Trooper and a snort from the other end of the barn. Music to Jesse's ears. Maybe that's why he chose this for his special spot to pray.

He dropped to his knees in the fresh shavings and laid his Stetson beside him. He inhaled the scent of pine wood in the dark cubicle, and then bowed his head.

Lord, what's happening in this dream? What are You saying to me? You know I hate that name and You know why. Donny's took to calling himself Thorn—and now I have this dream. Father God, if you've got anything to say about this, say it clear. Help me to hear You.

Jesse stayed still, quieted his thoughts and waited. Desperation drove him to wait, expecting an answer—something!

His knees began to feel their age. Exhaustion, after two nights of disturbed sleep, tried to tell him to go to bed. The cold began to penetrate, but he refused to budge. He really had no idea how long he'd waited, but when the answer came, he knew without a doubt what it was.

Forgive him.

Those words rose up from inside of him crystal clear and all he could feel at hearing this answer was pure anger. All he understood at the moment was that God was telling him to forgive his father. His and Donny's drunkard, cheater, abusive, deserter father. He refused to think of him as *dad*. He never had been a dad. He'd simply fathered two boys. No more than a sperm donor. He wasn't worth forgiving.

He bent low, his face nearly touching the shavings on the stall floor. He hugged his stomach with both arms feeling sick and wishing he'd never heard that answer.

Finally he rose up bracing himself with both hands in the wood chips. "*Lord, I can't forgive him. I can't.*"

Jesse groaned with long pent up anger and pain. The pain was as fresh as if the old man was standing right there in the horse stall with him, sneering. The groans of anguish kept coming until he finally spent himself. He straightened up, but stayed on his knees, his shoulders slumped with emotional exhaustion.

Nothing had ever felt so backward. So unfair. Every cell in his being was screaming in rebellion against this position God had put him in. Because it was the Lord's idea...no, His *command*, he had no way to fight against it. He knew that, but his insides were waging war anyway. His mind, even his physical body, wanted to jump up and hit something or somebody. At the same time, from deep inside him, a desire to obey what God wanted was fighting to be recognized.

0 Then the atmosphere changed—just that fast! He felt his body relax, his taut muscles sagged in relief. Then he realized his mind had calmed. His raging hate-filled thoughts stopped their torture. The air around him where he was still kneeling became lighter, easy to breathe. It came into him then that this was his moment, a moment of God's pure grace and peace

where he was given an inner strength to do what he had to do. And there in that moment, he chose to forgive his father.

When you seek me with all your heart—you will find me.

A lifelong battle was over. The pain and the turmoil oozed out of him. He thought he could feel it leaving.

"My Lord and my God," he whispered.

He didn't move and only barely breathed. He didn't want to disturb the sweetness of the atmosphere around him. He had heard Donny say that he'd felt the presence of God at times. Was this what he meant? Was His very presence here now? Jesse closed his eyes and soaked himself in whatever Heavenly experience he was enjoying. He had the sensation of floating—couldn't feel the ground under his knees. But then from the inside of him rose up words of praise and thanksgiving to the Lord Jesus. It poured out of him, but he couldn't tell if he was speaking out loud or just loudly thinking.

When he opened his eyes, everything was normal, except that his face was wet with tears and he still had that lightness in his soul. He had no clue, until this minute how imprisoned he had been by entertaining all those years of hatred for his dad. He was being set free. Truly free.

It was 5 am when he crawled back under the mound of quilts and curled his long muscled arms and legs around his sleeping little wife. His heart was nearly exploding with a fresh and intense love for her. Until now he didn't think it was possible to love her more. This was God's kind of love, a supernatural love, and he was awed and humbled at the fill-up he'd been given.

He stroked Laura's hair, kissed her bare shoulder and rubbed his hands up and down her arm. *Let us grow old together, Lord, and bless our kid's lives with this kind of love.*

She rolled over toward him. "Hey, is everything all right?"

"It is. Nothing's ever been so all right." He caressed her cheek lightly with his knuckles and closed his eyes a few seconds. When he opened them, she was searching his face. "I thought I knew, Laura. I thought that was all there was to being a Christian—a good husband to you, father to our kids, church on Sunday, work hard all week and pray every day." He became silent and stared past her face into the darkened room.

"I don't understand, Jess. You do all of those things and so well. You're a wonderful Christian man."

He looked at her then and even in the shadowy darkness she could see the radiance in his face. He was in awe of whatever had happened to him.

"There's more to knowing God than just those things. I felt His presence tonight in the barn. It seemed like I heard Him speak. I knew what He was saying. I've never known anything, *anything* like that before."

"What did you go out there for?"

"To pray. I kept having this dream over and over and I felt desperate to understand it. A scripture came to my mind—*When you seek Me with all your heart, you will find Me.* I couldn't get off the floor of the barn. Or I *wouldn't.* All I know for sure is I never felt so desperate for God as I did tonight."

Jesse described what he'd experienced a short time ago. They both were teary-eyed by the time he finished. They snuggled under the bed covers and wrapped up like one person instead of two. Sleep came immediately.

It was Thanksgiving Day. Reeny climbed out of bed just before sun-up to start the coffee. Donny was still holding that deep sleep breathing rhythm.

After making her way to the bathroom and back, she settled on the loveseat and soaked up the peacefulness of the morning. The small blaze in the fireplace seemed to be happy to be here too as she watched it dance.

She could hardly believe she had been here over two months already. Doctors had released her and Thorn both and they could take on whatever life brought.

She had to get use to the fact that she was married to Donny Brandon instead of Thorn. No one called him Thorn, except her, and he decided one day a couple weeks ago that he wanted her to call him Donny. He'd told her about his dad and the name, Thorn, but he had no idea why he started using it when he met her. Whatever crisscross the wiring had done in his head that day in Albuquerque, it must have straightened out, because he didn't want to be Thorn anymore. She shook her head on that thought. She loved Donny—the name and the man.

"Hey, woman! I smell coffee. Why haven't you served me yet?"

Still sitting with her back to him, she grabbed the big throw pillow beside her and slowly turned around. Bed covers still covered his head. She tip toed to the bed holding her breath so he wouldn't hear. She stood up on the top step beside the bed, pillow raised over his head for the attack. When he let out a deep unholy bellow and sat straight up, she screamed as loud as he did and slung her weapon through the air. In one swoop, he had her rolled up in his arms and flattened beneath him.

"You are gonna *have* to brush up on your *I gotcha's,* lady. You couldn't sneak up on a cemented fence post." He could feel her heart pounding against his chest. "I gotcha good, didn't I."

"You didn't scare me. I was ready for you."

He burst out laughing. "Yeah? I can't wait to catch you off guard. I'll need to get that on film."

A grin spread across her face. "Keep it up, smart boy. I'm planning a biggie for you. Just watch your back."

He let his forehead rest on hers. "Oh man, that ought to be good. You're on!" Then he kissed her hard and moved to lay against her side. There was nothing he wanted to do more at this minute, except peel that confining robe off of her and everything else underneath it. He knew she was physically healed now, but whether she was emotionally ready to make love with him—. Would she let him know?

"You have my heart, Reeny. I'll always be here."

She turned toward him and put a hand on his stubble roughened jaw, then leaned in and kissed him. “Ready for coffee?”

“If that’s all you’re offering, I’ll take it.”

She smiled at her next thought, knowing she shouldn’t say it, but couldn’t help herself.

“Well, you’re getting turkey at your brother’s house in a little while.”

It took about two seconds for that to sink in. In the same two seconds, she rolled over to escape the bed, but not fast enough. He caught the edge of her terry robe as she rolled and stripped it off both shoulders. He slung it away.

“Come here, you little vixen.”

Her feet missed the step-up beside the bed and the momentum sent her sprawling to the floor.

“Oh, no.” One leap and he was off the bed kneeling beside her. “Reeny, baby?” She didn’t move. He checked her pulse, and then looked under her closed eyelids. Then he stood and let out a shout to end all shouts. “Yeah! She’s out cold! I get all the coffee.” He took off to the kitchen making all the noise he could as he poured two cups.

She raised up then and yelled behind him. “Watch your back, cowboy. The biggie’s coming!”

Her eyes twinkled in answer to his laughter as they met for coffee on the loveseat, her robe securely wrapped back around her.

By noon, Jesse and Laura had a full house. Besides the three Brandon kids, Gramps and Granny Walton, Les and Kaitlyn Kane, Donny and Reeny and Judd, Toni and Abby Luke made up the Thanksgiving dinner list. The Lukes had hosted a huge holiday shindig at their place for all the ranch hands just two days earlier.

The weather was unusually warm for the high country at Thanksgiving. The kids ran in and out, the men conveniently had cowboy stuff to do in the barn while the women cooked, joked, laughed, grated and chopped.

Reeny had viewed scenes like this on TV, not realizing such places and families actually existed. She couldn't think of a better reason to be thankful today, or any day. She wondered if any of the women she was standing in the kitchen with knew what they had. She watched as they all shared, hugged and laughed together with real emphasis on each other—bragging on each other's children or accomplishments. She figured they *must* know how precious and special all of their lives were. It was obvious because they nurtured it well.

Reeny had picked up two sidekicks during the morning. Anna Leigh Brandon and Abby Luke clung to her like a new found playmate. She sneaked them licks from the chocolate pudding bowl and gave them the mashed potato beaters. She was their hero.

Finally when Granny Martha's loud mouth cut the air to the barn, the men hurried their appetites through the kitchen door.

"Okay, listen up. Here's the plan," Laura announced. "Everybody fix a plate and head for the patio just outside. There's enough chairs to get around the tables. Just pick you a spot."

Almost in unison, all the men removed their hats. No one moved, but waited for someone to turn thanks.

Laura looked at Jesse. "Honey, would you…"

"It's Reeny's turn," Anna Leigh interrupted her mom.

All eyes went to the little girl, then to Reeny. She was stunned and a little embarrassed. She had never prayed where anybody could hear her.

Laura tried to rescue her without making an issue of it. "Anna, we'll let Reeny do it the next time."

"No. She has to," she persisted. "It's her turn. Okay, Aunt Reeny?"

Reeny looked at the girl and nodded without realizing what she did.

As everyone bowed their heads, Reeny felt Anna grasp her hand and Abby took hold of her other one. Then she realized everyone had grasped the hand of whoever was next to them. Her heart was pounding and she had no idea what to say. Suddenly words breezed through her mind—*it's Thanksgiving. Just say thank-You to God.*

Finally, she managed to unlock her jaw and haltingly pray, *"Jesus, we want to say thank You for…for…every single thing You've done for us. Amen.*

Everybody said *amen* behind hers and when she looked up, nobody moved for a few seconds. Tears had filled every eye in the room.

That afternoon, Reeny decided it would be a good time to talk to the group of women about an idea she'd been entertaining a few days. They all seemed to be so close and concerned with each other's lives.

The kids were napping, the men were preoccupied with whatever was so important in the barn.

So much seemed to be coming up around the Christmas holiday. She didn't know if she could get any help with her project. Les and Kaitlyn had a wedding anniversary coming up. The birth of Toni and Judd's second baby was due. And then, it was Christmas with all that entailed for these families. She'd only had enough time to mention her idea when Granny Martha got up and peeped around the privacy wall of the patio.

"Reeny, doll, I believe you're about to get your cowgirl on."

She jumped up, the others following, to look around the wall. Donny was leading two tacked-out horses. He stopped a few steps from the ladies, grinning like a bird fed cat. He draped both sets of reins over his shoulders and lifted his hat just enough to pull a piece of paper out from under it. He opened it slowly, squinting like he could barely make out what it said.

"Let's see here. Believe it says, Mrs. Ree…Ree-ny Brandon. Yep, that's it. Says here you signed up for my horseback riding class."

"I did not," she chuckled nervously. The thought scared her. "Sure you did." He looked at the paper again.

The women were all trying to stifle laughter, knowing Donny to be the ranch prankster.

"Come see this. Says it right here."

Reeny walked out and took the paper. After she scanned the writing on it, her face burned. It read, *Git on this horse or I'm gonna kiss your face off right here in front of everybody.*

At her reaction, they all knew he'd written her a private message. But they laughed just the same.

"Donny, you oughta be ashamed," Martha scolded through her chuckles.

"Those ponies are ones the kids ride, Reeny," Laura offered. Take a ride. You'll love it. They won't go faster than a walk."

"Oh, well I just fed em some 747 jet fuel. Their raring to go. Look at em."

"Donny, really!" Toni was laughing out loud.

He stretched a wide grin, shifted his eyes and tapped the paper in her hands with his finger.

She looked up at the two sleepy looking horses flanking each side of her wacko husband and squared her shoulders—petrified shoulders. Sleepy or not, she'd never been on a horse. But she really wanted to. It was just a little confusing that she could feel so excited at the idea of riding and be scared to death at the same time.

"Okay, but you get on my horse first so I can see what he does."

"Why, I'd be happy to demonstrate little Poncho for you, Miz Brandon."

"That's intelligence for you," piped Granny Martha.

"Thank ya, Granny."

"I was meaning Reeny, Mister funny pants."

Donny dropped the reins of the horse on his far side and gathered up the others. He stuck his left foot in the stirrup and mounted up. Poncho didn't move. He stood relaxed and unconcerned.

He stepped down. "Your turn. Come on, I'll help you up." He held his arm out and with her heart racing, she let him help her into the saddle. With the reins in her right hand and her left holding a death grip on the saddle horn, she took her first horseback ride around the ranch yard.

They walked their horses side by side, around the barn and through the gate that led to their cabin.

Reeny's eyes were bright with excitement. Donny remembered well how he'd felt on his first ride. Just like she looked now.

He stopped his horse, Poncho automatically doing the same. He stood in his stirrups and leaned over toward her until he could plant a quick kiss on her lips. He pulled back enough to see her face clearly. She was looking him in his eyes, a look of sweet passion swirling in a way he'd not seen on her. Slowly he leaned in again and this time their lips met with a mutual passion that took them both by surprise. He put a hand behind her head and scrunched her hair in his fist, the pressure of his hold deepening the kiss until she forgot they were on horses. About the time he sensed she needed to come up for air, he felt her body sway toward him and unlocked his lip hold.

“Take your feet out of the stirrups,” he growled against the side of her mouth.

“What stirrups?”

“The ones your feet are stuck in.”

When she complied, he lifted her up and set her side saddle in front of him, then turned her in his arms and kissed her again. She reached her arms around his neck and pulled him closer, returning his kiss with a wildness she’d never felt in herself. She didn’t fully understand the passion racing her heartbeat, but she wanted more. She wanted to be closer to him than was physically possible. There was no way to get any closer. Yet she pulled him tighter, kissed him harder and wanted to climb inside of him.

A thought struck him then. Was this the *biggie* she had planned for him? A passionate joke? He pulled back enough to look into her face. *Nope!* She wasn’t putting him on. This girl was on fire!

“Donny,” she groaned, but the trembling question in her voice gave him pause.

-336“It’s okay, angel girl. You’re safe. You can be any way you want to be with me. Feel what you need to feel.”

She buried her face in his shirt front. “I can’t get close enough. I can’t hold you tight enough.”

He wanted to laugh with pure joy at this, but he swallowed it. He knew there were more than just her hormones raging out of control. *That,* of course, but fear was mixed up with it. Fear of losing the first good thing she'd probably ever had in her life—his family and all their friends. She trusted him and knew she was accepted and loved here. She knew *he* loved her and she was just afraid of losing that.

He wrapped both arms around her and pressed her as tight as he could against him. He held her that way, tight and secure for a long while. Neither of the horses moved a step.

"Reeny, I'm not going anywhere," he whispered against her hair. I love you plumb to the moon and back. This is your home. And, make no mistake about it, young lady, I want to make mad passionate love to you, over and over and over again. But I want you to be sure that you're ready for that step. I'm not rushing you and I don't want you to rush yourself."

"Oh, Donny, how I feel sometimes…it hurts my insides."

"I know." He entwined his fingers in her hair and gently pulled her head back until she turned her face up to his. He grinned down at her. "Think you can stand to look at this handsome face for the next fifty, sixty years?"

She squinted her eyes thoughtfully a moment. "Oooh, yuck."

He looked wounded. "What do you mean oooh yuck?"

She laughed. "Oh, not you. I just tried to imagine *me* in sixty years."

"Yeah right. Got yourself out of that one right quick, didn't ya, slick."

The smile that spread her mouth instantly twinkled her eyes. "Deal with it, cowboy. You've got forty years."

He tipped his head back and laughed, loving these glimpses of the woman he married—the real Reeny. He knew that once she bloomed all the way open, she was going to give him a run for his fun-loving money. He loved it!

He claimed her mouth again, and then moved to her nose, cheeks, and eyes and back to her lips.

Her giggles broke up the moment just in time to give him enough sense to feel his horse stiffen a split second before charging forward. He tightened his hold around Reeny and grabbed up the reins simultaneously.

"Whoa, Buddy, easy."

Poncho had already charged on, but stopped a short distance when his equine sidekick stopped.

Donny heard a motor idling a distance behind them. He turned Buddy around and saw Jesse sitting on the four-wheeler where he remained still and waited for him to get his horse under control. These two ponies were not afraid of motor vehicles, but jumped at the surprise that rushed up behind them.

Reeny, on the other hand, had a death grip on Donny's tonsil, her scream doing as much to scare their mounts as Jesse's intrusion.

"Okay, Annie Oakley," he laughed. Then he coughed and bugged out his eyes and stuck out his tongue. "You can let go now," he gagged. I saved you. You're choking your hero."

"Oh man! What happened?"

“Company drove up. Calm down. We’re under control.”

When she released her grip, he rose up in the stirrup and swung his other leg behind him and dismounted, keeping a hand firmly on her hip until he slid her to a soft landing to the ground.

Then Jesse drove his ATV up to where they stood and shut off the engine.

“Hey, brother.” Donny studied his face and knew he was bothered by something. Jesse had never been one to wear a façade across his thoughts.

“Sorry to interrupt you kids, but I had a phone call from the sheriff and this message can’t wait. They believe they’ve identified the other man involved in your kidnapping, Reeny. An APB went out after finding out he’d been gone from his home for the past week. He was recognized by the manager of a steak house located less than a hundred miles from here. He’s the Mayor of a small New Mexico town not far from where you grew up.”

Donny and Reeny both stared unblinking at Jesse.

“The sheriff is putting a deputy on patrol at our house and you two need to stay with us until this gets resolved.”

Donny nodded, and then put an arm around Reeny’s shoulders. “You okay?”

She jumped at the sudden touch that brought her back from a few moments of imagining that filthy excuse daring to come here and intrude on her new fairy tale life on this ranch—again! She wasn’t scared in the least. Mad, yes! In fact, she was furious that he would threaten the security of her family.

"Let the scumbag coward come. I think I could take him out with my bare hands."

She watched the brothers exchange surprised looks and she knew what they were thinking, so she added, "You know what they say about small packages, don't you?" With that, she stiffened her back, strode over to her horse and without a thought, mounted up and kicked the pony's sides like she was shown.

Donny nearly swallowed his tongue as he watched Jesse almost lose his fight to hold himself together.

Calmly and mostly straight faced, Donny walked over, gathered Poncho's reins off the ground and handed them to her with a wink.

She looked confused for a second, then, "Oh." Poncho strolled off with the next kick.

"Scumbag Coward better tread lightly," Donny quipped through his teeth while he mounted up and followed her back to the barn.

Jesse shook his head and let his laugh escape. "Never a dull moment," he muttered under his breath.

Reeny followed her nose, a strong smell of fresh coffee coming from Laura's kitchen. Jesse had taken Poncho to unsaddle and turn out for the night while Donny took care of Buddy. They both insisted she head inside and let the other women know they were back. She figured they just wanted her out of the way and the coffee smell sealed the deal.

"Hey, our new cowgirl is back," Martha grinned big and moved to pour her a cup, already knowing she was a coffee drinker. "Here you go." She picked up her own half full cup and pointed to the back door. "Let's sit out there. Too nice a day to be inside. Laura's getting babies ready for bed."

Reeny was stirred up inside and felt comforted at the chance to talk to Ms. Martha. She seemed like the 'mama' type—something Reeny had never known.

"So, how was it—the ride?"

"Oh, I can't wait til the next time." Her eyes danced with real excitement.

Martha chuckled. "Tell me that again in a couple days. The first ride will make you walk funny. It's called saddle sore."

"Well, I may not get to go again for a while. Donny and I are staying here under guard of a sheriff's deputy. They think the creep that…that hurt me…is in the area."

Martha straightened and looked away in intense thought, a solemn expression settling in her eyes. "Is that right?"

Reeny nodded, watching her.

"So, they think he's coming back here…to get to you?"

"Yes. I'm really sorry for all this."

"Nothing for you to be sorry for, honey. You're in a good place here." She stood up, not sure what she should do. She had seen Jesse talking to Hank just a little while ago. She couldn't hear their conversation, but Hank had turned a raging shade of red and had Jesse tell her he'd be back for her later. Then he left in the truck, the same time Jesse rode off on the four-wheeler. Something was brewing and she was afraid she might know what it was. She could feel it.

"Reeny, you stay put now. We don't need nothing happening to you." Martha stepped around the table and gathered her up in a tight hug. "Don't be sorry for being here. You belong to us now and we all love you." She straightened and turned to leave. "Tell Laura I had to go home." She disappeared around the patio enclosure and headed toward the barn.

In less than five minutes, Jesse passed by in his dually taking her home.

"Thanks for the ride." Martha stepped down off of the truck step-rail in front of her and Hank's cabin.

"You bet. Are you sure everything's all right?"

"Yep. Save us a couple pieces of that chocolate pie." She slammed the truck door and waved him off.

He laughed. *She's got to be kidding. If I find a crumb left over, it's mine!*

Hank was sitting at the kitchen table when she walked in. Even though she half expected it, her heart bumped an extra jolt in her slender chest when she saw it.

Without a word, she started a pot of coffee. For five minutes she kept her back to Hank. Neither spoke until she put two steaming cups on the table and sat down across from him.

There was the box. It was opened and the contents laid out on the small dining table. A holster holding a revolver lay in front of Hank, a badge on one side of it and a yellowed newspaper clipping. A second equally aged paper clipping lay face up on top of the gun—a picture of a man and woman and their joint obituary write up. *Henry and Jill Rhea.*

"I know you've already seen these," he said quietly.

Surprised, she nodded. "I ran across the box up in the closet a couple years ago. I thought I put it back like you had it."

"You did. You forgot to put the dust back over your fingerprints."

"That was a hard thing that happened, Hank."

"Yes, mam." He cut a sideways glance at her. "I see the questions. What do you want me to tell you?"

"Guess I'm curious about how you went from that, to chuck wagon cook for these ranches. And do the boys know about this?"

"Always was a good cook. My mother made sure of that. Daddy taught me to cowboy. Job here was open. They were kinda desperate for a *decent* cook." He chuckled at that. "Answer to your other question is no."

She swallowed hard. This was a side of Hank Walton she'd never even glimpsed. His sweet, low voiced demeanor was what had attracted her to him years back. There was shortness with hard undertones just under the surface. His effort to hold it in was lacking. She'd always sensed there was more to Hank than was showing, but didn't care what it was. She fell in love with the dude ranch cook and that was that. Whatever this stuff all over the table meant, she'd just have to deal. She loved him.

"What else?" he asked simply.

"What's your plan for this? You going after that pervert that's threatening Reeny?"

"Sounds like he's comin' to me. This is our family, Martha. He gets in my space to threaten mine...I'll be ready."

Carefully she picked up the fragile obit and studied the couple's picture then put it back on top of the gun. "You're trying to feel responsible for their deaths, aren't you?"

"I *am* responsible. Thought I was a real hero until I seen what it cost those two."

"So...are you going to carry that gun around with you?"

He hesitated a long minute before answering.

"Martha, I think the less you know about this, the better. If the time comes where I need to step up, I'll be ready. Leave it at that, all right?"

They searched each other's eyes, deeply imploring understanding.

"You know I'll worry about you."

"I figured you would. I'm getting old, hon, and some days I feel it more than others, but I'm not *that* old. I mostly humor them boys, after doing so much *chuck wagon cook* acting for the kids and greenhorn guests that come out here. It's easy to get in that character and stay there when you live it day in and day out." He smiled across the table at her. "I can handle whatever I need to."

She nodded. "I know you can." The lump grew so big in her throat, she couldn't say any more.

After a glance out the window at the setting sun, he got up and closed and locked the front door, closed the kitchen window blind, then turned around and leaned down to plant a kiss on his wife's lips.

"It took me most of my life to find a wife, but I sure got a good un," he said against her mouth.

She pulled back slightly and took a breath. "Yes, you did and unless you want somebody else to have this *good un*, you better keep yourself in one piece!"

"He laughed out loud as he grabbed her hand and pulled her up and toward the bedroom.

The Brandon brothers were up before dawn the next morning. Both were hired out to the Double OO during the dude ranch down time and they had a long few miles of fence to check today.

Jesse filled a thermos and two large mugs with hot coffee and then tossed a package of cinnamon rolls onto the kitchen island. "This ought to hold us til lunch. Since Hank's working the chuck wagon, we'll get fed good then." He pulled himself a couple rolls out of the package and laughed when Donny balanced five of them in one hand and his coffee mug in the other on the way out the door.

"What!" He stopped and looked back at his brother like he was offended.

"Nothin. Get out of here before we wake up the house."

"Yeah, you're just jealous cause you get fat and I don't."

"Uh huh, wait a few years, kid."

The barn was still dark, but Hank's truck was parked by the door.

"What's he doing here so early?" Donny mumbled through a mouthful of a doughy roll.

"Hey, boys."

They both jerked their heads toward the back of the barn toward the end of the petting zoo pens. Hank's silhouette blended with the black of night. His heavy, short, black jacket and black Stetson, rather than his old straw, gave him an image of someone trying to conceal himself in the dark. Only his pickup and voice made him recognizable.

"Hank?" Jesse looked around and spied the patrol car partially hidden under the darkness of trees beside one of the guest cabins. "Everything all right?" He made his way over to him?

"I couldn't sleep. Thought I'd help watch the place for a few hours. I know that deputy's out there, but an extra set of eyes and ears couldn't hurt."

"No, sir, it won't hurt a bit. Thank you, Hank." Jesse shook his hand and patted him on the shoulder. "See you at noon."

The Brandon's checked on the horses in the barn and petting zoo animals, then loaded up and headed for the Double OO.

"What do you make of that, Jesse? I haven't seen Hank out of his beat up old straw since I've known him, except when we put on a shindig for the dudes in summer. And I've never seen that jacket on him either."

Jesse yawned and reached for the thermos he'd propped on the seat. He handed it to Donny. "Here, pour me a shot. I don't know, except he looked really riled when I told him about that New Mexico mayor being seen in this area." He took the coffee. "Fact is, I've never seen him get mad like that. Didn't know he had it in him. Looked mean as an old grizzly protecting her cubs."

"Maybe that was it. We're all his family. His protecting instincts kicked in over this mess. I can understand that." Donny poured himself another hot swallow from the thermos.

Jesse nodded and took a sip. "Well, I didn't sleep much last night myself. Me and the Lord visited for most of it."

"Same here, Jess. In fact, I believe He spoke to me last night."

They were quiet as Jesse pulled in and parked the dually on the side of Judd's barn. He stared at Donny. "So…you going to tell me what He said."

He looked up at his brother. "*Trust Me.* That's what He said. *Trust Me.*"

Jesse tightened the top on the thermos. "We can do that, little brother. And, by the way, I've been meaning to ask you, how come Reeny is calling you Donny now instead of Thorn?"

"I asked her to." He was thoughtful a moment. "That was a strange deal. I introduced myself to her as Thorn and wondered why I did. Then just a while back, I didn't like the sound of it anymore."

Jesse stared at nothing out the windshield. He knew what had happened. God had given *him* a thorn until he became willing to repent of his hatred and forgive their dad. He smiled. Who could figure God out?

***

CHAPTER TEN

"Donny Brandon! You bow-legged thief! You give that back!" Reeny screeched at his back while she chased his sorry hide across the brown grassy patch in front of the ranch house. "Tackle him, Andy!"

Before Andy could get up any momentum, Anna Leigh darted across the yard and cut him off. Andy changed tactics mid-stride, grabbed her up and carried her in the chase. Reeny beat the pack to the tackle when she lunged for Donny's hips, wrapped her arms tight around him and brought him down, face to the ground. She kept a tight hold until Andy set his offended baby sister on his back.

"Get him, Anna," Reeny yelled. "Make him give it back."

Anna Leigh was small for a four year old, but she could hold her own with the rest of them. Her fingers spread around both sides of his neck as far as she could stretch them and squeezed. "Cough it up, Uncle Donny. Right now!"

"Yeah, *Uncle* Donny. Say *uncle* and give it back." Reeny bit him on the back of his leg and he knew it was all over.

"All right...uncle...uncle!" He pulled the little pink Nerf football out from underneath him and held it up over his shoulder for the little monkey on his back to take.

Anna snatched it and ran off giggling to hide behind her big brother.

Laughing, Reeny and Donny got up and brushed off.

"Y'all women are savages. I could have been severely kilt."

"You needed a good killing, stealing that baby's Nerf ball." Reeny scolded through her chuckles and short breath.

Laura stuck her head out the front door. "Has anyone noticed that the north front's here. It's getting dark and cold."

The kids went inside while Donny piggy backed his scrappy little bride back to their cabin. The pair had moved into the nearest guest cabin across the drive from the ranch house.

It had been a couple days since her abductor had been spotted in the area. The deputy had to be pulled off of his nightly guard duty for other pressing duties.

The ranch remained on high alert. The front entrance gate was pad locked each night, something Jesse had never done before.

Hank continued his own surveillance at night, demanding that Martha sleep at the Brandon's.

Mayor Raul Heinz had been identified through photographs by Reeny as her captor, the one she had known only as Sir. He was missing and on the priority wanted list nationwide. The fear was that he had escaped the U.S., but so far nothing had come up on his passport.

Jesse had been increasingly concerned about Hank. His self-implored night watch job appeared to be taking a toll on the older gentleman. He had become quieter than usual—moody and sullen. Not the Hank he had known for years.

He had watched Donny head inside his cabin, engaged in his usual horseplay with Reeny. He couldn't help but laugh at their antics which was more common than not. Nothing like young love, or the older variety either, for that matter.

About the time they shut the cabin door behind themselves, Hank emerged in his dark hat and jacket and found a dark spot beside the barn to hang out. Jesse figured this would be a good time to approach him about whatever was really going on with him. It hadn't been that big of an issue until this morning when he caught a glimpse of a handgun in the back waistband of his jeans. *Now* it was time to talk.

Armed with two smoking mugs of coffee, he made his way through the bite of the north wind to Hank's perch at the back end of the barn. From this spot, Jesse knew he could see the ranch house, Donny's cabin and the road that went out to the Honeymoon Hideout. His surveillance of the ranch was a serious thing for him. He handed over a cup.

"Thanks, Jesse."

"You sure you want to sit out in this cold?"

"I'm fine. Dressed for it."

"You know we all appreciate what you're doing, Hank. Creeps like Heinz are unpredictable and deadly. But, you can't take these all-nighters much longer without some repercussion."

He didn't look at Jesse, but nodded his head, knowing he couldn't rest until the filth was caught.

"Hank, I have to ask you about that pistol stuck in your waistband. Had no idea you were packin."

Hank faced him then. He figured he might have seen it this morning. He wasn't sure until now. "Well, I knew this was coming sooner or later. Might should have told you, but there was too much at stake if it got out." He unzipped a pocket on the inside of his bulky jacket and carefully pulled the newspaper clippings out. He handed them both to Jesse. "Go read these and then we'll talk."

Without a word, Jesse turned and headed for the barn. Inside the tack room he turned on a small lamp and sat down on a hay bale against the back wall. He could tell the paper was old and he unfolded it with care. Inside was a second clipping of a picture of a middle aged couple. He read : *A joint memorial service for Henry and Jill Rhea—*

He scanned the obituary, not recognizing any names. They were survived by one child, Buck Rhea. He figured they must have died together, some thirty years ago.

He lay that aside and read the second clipping: *Parents of a rookie police officer who was involved in the fatal shooting of a well-known gang leader, Karl Garcon, were found shot to death in their isolated farmhouse. Officer Buck Rhea, on the force less than a year, stumbled onto what turned out to be one of the largest drug deals in progress…*

He read the entire article twice. The couple in the obit was obviously the parents of this rookie that shot the gang leader. He jerked his head up at the realization of what this might be. These people were close friends or family to Hank. The clippings were out of a newspaper in California. Was Hank from out there? He had always been quiet and closed mouth about himself.

He got up, turned off the lamp and went back to talk to Hank. He handed back the clippings and waited until he zipped them back up in his jacket.

"I read the story. That was a terrible deal." Jesse rested his hands in his back jeans pockets and rocked back on his heels.

Hank stared off into space. His face was shadowed by the darkness, but Jesse could still see the heavy thinking going on by his expression.

"I take it you knew the people involved in that?"

Hank turned and faced him—looked him in the eye. "My name is Buck Rhea."

A long beat passed as they stared at each other. Jesse finally exhaled, but couldn't find a question or a statement inside his head just yet. He heard Hank begin talking, but his voice wasn't right. It was stronger and gruffer-toned than Hank's.

"I'd only been on the force for ten months. I was patrolling about 2am when I turned a corner. My headlights hit a group of men. Next thing I knew I was being shot at. I called for backup and I remember firing my gun. Can't remember drawing it though. Next I knew, I woke up in an ambulance with EMT's telling me not to move. I'd been shot."

Jesse hadn't moved a muscle, not even his eyes off of Hank's face.

After a moment's pause, he continued. "Before I got out of the hospital, I learned who I had shot and killed at the same time they told me my folks had been murdered. A message was left in black marker on the wall over where their bodies lay. Said Buck Rhea was next. The way that all finished up was, I went into witness protection. I don't know if I would have allowed that or not now, but at the time, I was young, guilt-ridden and well, I was out of it for a while. They'd already buried my mother and dad. I never got to see their graves. By birth and blood, I'm Buck Rhea. But he died thirty years ago. Legally and for the rest of my life, I'm Hank Walton."

Jesse blinked a couple of times as if to shake loose from his fixed-stare shock.

Finally. "Mercy, Hank."

"I know. Maybe I should have leveled with you at some point. Guess I didn't know how after all this time and I would understand if you thought it best I move on."

"Does Martha know any of this?"

He nodded slowly. "She found my gun and badge I kept…and the newspapers. Found the box I kept them in a long time ago, but she never said anything about it."

Jesse understood the passion he had been displaying the past nights, watching out for his wife and children as much as for Reeny. He suspected that beneath the sweet, soft spoken exterior of this cowboy cook and Gramps to his kids, lay smoldered long buried pain and anger. That's what he had seen on Hank's face the day he told him Reeny's kidnapper was spotted back in this area.

A lump bunched up in his throat. Hank Walton obviously lived in a world of emotional pain and there wasn't anything he could do to help. He knew him to be a Godly praying man and knew that was how he had managed to possess the kind, loving character he'd always displayed to everyone.

He put a hand on Hank's shoulder and squeezed. "I'm truly sorry about what happened to your parents. There's not an adult living in this world who doesn't have a past they'd just as soon never happened. Yours holds more heartache than a man ought to have to bear. But know this, Hank…" Jesse swallowed hard, his voice breaking. "My family here is your family. God Almighty brought you here to give you something back of what you lost, in the only way possible. He even added a few grandkids to boot."

Hank didn't move. His arms hung by his sides as a tear trailed down his gray whiskered face. "Thank you, Jesse. God did real good for me."

Donny leaned his head back on the couch and closed his eyes. A small flame peeked around the gas logs in the fireplace. He listened to the sounds of the shower only a few steps behind his head. His little bride was in there, not a stitch on and all he could do about it was visualize the picture, like he'd been doing for weeks. He didn't think she had a clue what kind of control he'd had to exert over himself every night while she curled up in his arms to sleep. Just keeping his hands away from her intimate places was pushing the envelope of *not giving him more than he could bear.*

He believed she loved him, at least on some level. At times she seemed to be eager for more of his caresses, but he always sensed a pulling back if he tried to cross a line she'd drawn for herself.

He got that. Her past was something he had to continuously be aware of. When she was ready for more, she'd let him know. That was the only way he could look at this. He couldn't...wouldn't take a chance on causing her more trauma. He loved her too much for that. But his resolve was wearing on him more than ever.

There had always been the fear that she would cling to him for the sake of having a home and people to call family. He didn't believe real love could be *worked up.* There was a chemistry of some kind that when mixed together, a fire would explode inside of both of them. Just the sight of each other would ignite it. That's what he had felt for Reeny from the start. He'd fallen stupid in love with her in Albuquerque, and he'd keep her safe from this sicko that was obsessed with her if it cost him his life. God had put him in this position, yes, but he *wanted* to be here for her. She had something that belonged to him. She had his heart.

Lost in his mental ramblings it took him a minute to realize the shower wasn't running and there was no sound coming from the bathroom. He listened intently. Nothing. He jumped up and stood at the bathroom door.

"Reeny?"

Silence.

He grabbed the knob and turned, cracking the door open. "Reeny?"

At no response, he jerked the door open. She stood in the center of the small space outside of the shower, frozen in place and staring at the uncovered window pane. She held a tight grip on the towel wrapped around her. Her hair was pinned loosely on top of her head. He squeezed in on the side of her to see her mouth open and fear holding her in shock.

He grasped her upper arm and gave her a slight shake. "Reeny, what happened? What's wrong?"

She clutched his shirt front and cried out. "He's out there. I saw him in the window. I saw his face in the window." Her towel dropped to the floor around her feet as she grabbed Donny with both hands. He pulled her damp body against him and tried to calm her trembling. He glanced up at the foggy glass panes. His first thought was that she had to be mistaken. Even if someone was out there, she couldn't have seen him through that.

Her grip on his t-shirt was about to pull it off of him and she was twisting around as though to pull out of his grip. Then he realized she was trying to use him to hide from the sight of the window.

Her towel was on top of his boots. He lifted one foot up enough to grasp it, then he jerked it up and rewrapped her. He turned her enough to get her moving through the door and to the couch. A quick twist of the knob near the bottom of the fireplace front brought up a higher blaze.

"Sit still. I'm going to get your clothes." He grabbed a bulky white terry robe from the small hall closet and tossed it to her. "Wrap up in this," then headed for the front door. "I'm going to look around."

He knew the bathroom and bedroom windows were securely locked. He'd made sure of that the day they moved in.

Outside, he reached above the door frame and grasped the tire iron he'd hidden on the ledge. Before he could head around to the back of the cabin, a figure stepped out from behind the wide base of a pine a few feet away. Donny stiffened and every muscle in his body was concentrated in the death grip he had on the tire iron.

"It's Hank, Donny." His voice was barely above a whisper, but Donny heard. He also saw the pistol in his hand and realized this might not have been just Reeny's imagination.

Both men stood stock still and listened intently for sounds of movement in the darkness around them. It was silent. Too silent. Hank motioned for Donny to stand still while he moved to the back of the cabin. Donny knew his weapon wasn't the best in this situation. He couldn't beat a bullet to death if it was coming at him.

After circling the house, Hank told him he'd seen what he thought could be a person, a large one, walking toward the back of the cabin.

Donny felt his blood chill. "Reeny thought she saw Heinz's face in the bathroom window not five minutes ago."

"Get her and take her across to Jesse's. Tell him to call the sheriff. Make sure everybody's inside over there."

Reeny had gotten dressed and was standing with her back against the front wall by the door so she could see every area of the cabin. The handle of a butcher knife from hell was locked into both of her hands. Fear…anger…murder was mixed together in her face.

He immediately calmed himself and spoke as matter of fact as he could. "Everything's all right, baby. Let me have that thing before you hurt me and let's walk across to the ranch house."

She didn't buy it. "He's out there, isn't he? That…that stinking, filthy, pig of a sorry excuse…that…"

She ran through a string of expletives on the end of her tirade that Donny was sure she was making up as she went. New ones on him! He reached to carefully take charge of the knife, but she jerked away.

"I'm keeping this and I hope the slimy son-of-a-"

"No, you're not carrying that thing. Let me have it."

She held it out to the side. "Leave me alone, Donny." Hysteria was taking her over.

Time was crucial and there wasn't any for this. He grabbed the wrist holding the knife and squeezed until she cried out and dropped it.

"He's out there! I saw him!" Her voice rose to just under a scream.

"I believe you." He pulled sharply on her wrist to stop her uproar. "We have to get Jesse and call the sheriff. We have to go—now." He spoke as calmly as he could.

Without another word, he put a protective arm around her, crossed the drive and barreled inside the back door.

Laura and Martha were finishing the dishes. Both turned around and froze, dishes and towel in hand, at the looks on their faces.

"Jesse?"

"In the office, Donny."

He took off in long strides down the hall. Martha and Laura emptied their hands and reached to comfort Reeny. She told them what she had seen in the window.

After a couple minutes, the two brothers came out heading for the back door. Jesse grabbed his hat and coat and tossed an extra down jacket to Donny before stepping out on the stoop to grab his boots and quickly scan the grounds.

He stepped into his boots, giving orders to Laura at the same time. "Get the kids and all of you stay in the playroom so I'll know where everybody is. It appears we have some uninvited company. Sheriff's on the way."

As soon as they were outside, Jesse pulled his Smith and Wesson .38 caliber revolver from inside of his shirt, loaded it, set the safety and stuck it in the side pocket of his coat. They found Hank leaned against the big pine by the cabin.

"I believe he's hidin out there, boys. I'd a heard him moving, big as they say he is."

"He's one brazen son-of-a-gun," Donny whispered gruffly. "He stared in the window at Reeny when she showered."

The screaming sirens and flashing red and blue got their attention and reminded Jesse that he'd forgotten to unlock the entrance gate.

"Keep your eyes peeled. Be right back." He ran for his truck and was back within two minutes. Four patrol cars wailed up the drive only a minute behind him.

At the same time, Laura ran from the house toward the barn yelling for Andy. He had gone out after supper to check on his lambs. The last time Jesse saw him, he was in his room, neck deep in school work. He thought she must have forgotten.

"Laura, wait!" Jesse ran behind her. Just as he reached the barn door, he heard her scream. It felt like a knife had plunged into his heart at the sound. He ran inside. Laura was several yards into the interior. When she heard him come in, she stretched her arm behind her, motioning him to stop. He looked past her to the dimly lighted far end and felt his heart slam into his chest. His son had a huge beefy arm holding him around his throat. A revolver was pressed against his temple.

Mother and son searched each other's face intently as if this moment might be their last to spend together.

Slowly she moved her eyes upward and looked the man squarely in his. They were eyes of bitterness and evil. A strange calm fell over her suddenly. She felt her tense muscles relax. All fear oozed away. It was other-worldly. She wasn't the least bit afraid of him. Slowly she walked toward him and her son.

"I'll kill him, lady," he shrieked at her. "You got what's mine. I want that girl back or I'll kill him."

Everyone outside had run toward the woman's scream and now were frozen silent, knowing a sudden move could set him off.

She kept walking, one slow step after another, never taking her eyes from the man's until she could touch her child.

"Mr. Heinz, let him go. I'll go with you. I'll be your girl now."

He seemed to be taken aback, the gentle softness of her voice confused him. His arm slackened and she jerked Andy away and pushed him hard off to the side. Instantly, the man grabbed her and placed her in the same choke hold.

"No!" Jesse panicked, fear almost making him light headed. He fought the fight of his life to stand still and not force this madman's hand.

"Go to Dad, Andy," she said softly. "Go on now."

Even seeing the gun pushed against his mother's head, he held himself in check and began to step backward toward Jesse.

Heinz was looking past the lineup of cowboys and cops toward the open barn door. He could see the flashing lights of the patrol cars. He knew this barn alley way circled all the way around to the next isle, the one where the door was standing open. He was big enough. There was a chance he could shoot his way through. But he didn't have the girl. They did. But he had one of theirs and they weren't giving him any choice. He had no choice!

He dragged Laura backward farther down the barn aisle with him until they were out of sight. Suddenly, he laughed—a loud, chilling guttural sound and shoved her to the ground.

Laura's strangled cry was mingled with the horrendous blast of the gun. Horses squealed and bucked and stomped in their stalls at the sudden explosive noise.

Jesse didn't remember moving from where he had been standing. His next recollection was sitting on the hay strewn floor holding his wife, rocking her in his arms. He glanced at Heinz's body sprawled lifeless in a heap down the aisle. Laura clung to him, shaking and reassuring him over and over that she was alright. She had been shoved down so hard that she rolled across the aisle up against a stall door a split second before the deafening roar had thundered on all sides of her.

"It's over now. It's over," Jesse tried to calm his wife as well as himself. He stood up and helped her to her feet.

He looked for whoever had done the shooting, but all the officers were as stunned and unsure as he and Donny.

Andy went to his mom and let her hold him for the first time in years.

Several deputies finally reacted, reaching for their holstered guns when Jesse jumped forward and put up his hand. "Hold on, hold on."

Hank stepped out of the shadows, his arm hanging down, a .44 magnum in his hand. His boots were gone. Sticks of hay were clinging to his sock feet.

Jesse knew what Hank had done. The two of them had built a small attic space for extra storage years ago. There was a vent on the roof barely large enough for a man to get through and a ladder attached to the wall behind a stack of hay bales that led from the barn into the attic. The small concave between the end stall and space for the hay was enough to conceal Hank's entrance into the barn from the top.

With tears in his eyes, Hank held the gun out to Jesse. He took it and handed it off to Donny, nodding slowly several times before he reached out and held his older friend with a knowing empathy.

Martha had a heck of a time keeping Reeny inside after Laura and Andy didn't come back.

"This is my fault. I brought all this mess to this ranch. It's my problem. I need to get out there and…"

"No you don't, young lady." Martha stood with her back against the playroom door. Both women whispered their frustrations, as the children had thankfully fallen asleep on quilts on the floor. "You were sent right here by the Lord Himself, Reeny Brandon. Don't you know that?"

"I've put everyone's lives in danger, Granny Martha. God didn't do that."

"Well, I beg to differ. I believe I heard the story told that God commanded Donny to marry you and bring you home. This was His plan all along."

Reeny went very still. Her stomach felt like a huge fist had just landed in it, knocking all the air out of her. She didn't say another word, but sat back down in the rocking chair where she'd rocked Jesse, Jr. to sleep a few minutes ago.

It had been several days since the shooting and everyone was pushing to get life back on its normal track. The drama and the trauma that had been experienced at High Point the past weeks were enough to last the whole gang for a long time.

Andy had agreed to visit and counsel with Pastor Judd, even though according to his young mind, he was fine.

Jesse, Donny and Hank all worked long hours for Judd Luke. Toni was due to give birth to their second baby and Judd was hanging close to the house.

Granny Martha spent the biggest part of each day helping Laura with the children.

No one spoke about the shooting, but it was noticed by the women that Reeny was staying away. She and Donny hadn't moved back to the Honeymoon Hideout, but stayed in the smaller cabin across the drive. The only time she was seen was walking to the barn during the day for an hour, maybe two, and then return to her cabin. They knew she needed some space after all she'd experienced, even before coming here with Donny.

Around noon when she came back out of the barn this time, she was leading Poncho. She mounted up and walked off toward the pasture gate at the back of the barn.

"Best thing in the world for her," Martha told Laura, as they watched her ride out of sight. With babies napping, it was coffee hour at the kitchen bar.

"Martha, what would we do without coffee?"

"Blow plumb up, I suspect."

The two had gotten acquainted over cups of coffee nearly seven years ago sitting at this same kitchen island. A lot had happened during those years. Mostly, life happened—some tragic, but most of it was happy times.

"I've been thinking." Laura looked off into space.

"Oh, that's scary! I remember one of your *thinking* times a few years ago. Bout got us both strung up."

They both laughed, remembering the time they did a re-do on Jesse's ranch when he was out of town. Laura was only a dude ranch guest at the time.

"Calm down. It's nothing that dramatic, I promise. Remember at Thanksgiving, Reeny mentioned a little surprise she wanted to do for Donny?"

She nodded.

"Maybe we could help her get that done. She wanted to get our family and friends together and have a real wedding ceremony."

"Oh, that would be fun." Martha got excited. "And just what they need, after everything else."

"It would be great fun. Sort of a new beginning for both of them."

Martha squinted her eyes. "Now, how are we going to make this ceremony be a surprise for Donny? That might be tough to pull off."

Laura gave her an impish smile. "What! For two old pros like us! I've been thinking about this for a while and I've got a plan. You'll like it."

Martha put her hand over her heart and wailed, "Oh, Lord help, here we go again." She paused a split second. "Okay! Spill the beans. I'm in."

Laura laughed out loud, then slapped her hand over her mouth, darting her eyes toward the kids' bedroom where they were sleeping.

She gave her the low-down on the plan and Martha teared up. "Love this all to pieces, girlfriend." She sniffled and touched the corners of her eyes with a paper towel. "When will this happen?"

"How about Christmas Eve?"

"Oh!" Fresh tears sprang up. She dabbed at them and laughed. "I'm as giddy as a kid on Christmas morning over this."

Laura's eyes glimmered wet, mostly watching Granny Martha's reaction. "Well then, let's get started. We'll get everyone else clued in first. Then, we'll go see Donny and Reeny."

With snow falling and the wind getting up, Jesse pulled the collar of his heavy coat up to help shield his neck. Donny seemed oblivious to the dropping temperature as he rode a short distance away. They were helping drive the Double OO's herd into close winter pasture for easier head count and feeding.

Jesse eased his mount over beside his too-quiet younger brother. "What are you thinking so hard about?"

Donny kept looking at the spot out in space he'd been staring at for too long. He mumbled, "Not a thing."

"Well, that thing you're not thinking about is letting those two renegades on your side of the drag run off."

Donny wheeled around and headed the hyper little yearlings back toward the herd, then rode back up beside Jesse.

After a silent minute, "Want to talk about it?"

Actually, he did, but they rode in silence for a while before he could arrange his words. He fiddled with his long, split reins and shoved his hat back and then forward again.

"It's Reeny. Ever since the night of the shooting, she's been, well, she won't talk or hardly look at me. If I try to touch her, she steps out of my reach."

He nodded, knowingly. "That young lady has been through more adversity than most will experience in their entire lifetime. Could be just catching up, being as it's all physically over with now. The horror of it all might be settling in."

Donny didn't respond. That was worth considering, he figured, but didn't feel altogether right. No, there was something more than that bothering her. He couldn't help but believe the problem was him. She was sure directing this attitude toward him.

"You don't think that's it, do you?"

He shook his head. "No, there's something else besides that. She's clung to me throughout this ordeal and now she's acting like I've done something wrong."

Jesse mulled that over a minute. "I know you didn't ask for any, but I'll give you a little *been there, done that* advice just the same. You and Reeny better learn right off to talk to each other. If you don't communicate, especially when problems come up between the two of you, you won't last fifteen more minutes."

Donny looked at him like he'd missed half of what he just told him about her behavior. "Now, how does that work when she won't talk to me?"

"Well, if it was me and Laura, I'd sit her down and stand in front of her until she told me why she was acting that way. That silent treatment can go on for days. Me and Laura learned to force the other one out of that nonsense."

Jesse noticed that something seemed to have hit home with him. After a minute, he watched Donny's back straighten, and then his shoulders lifted. No more was said about it.

Donny purposefully stayed away from the cabin until just after dark. He gave Reeny time to shower and get comfortable in her pj's before he went in to visit about their issue. Or at least, try and find out what the issue was.

He was thrilled to find out she had been saddling and riding Poncho on her own. He had hoped she would begin to develop a love for horses and his *ranchy* lifestyle. That would be a bonus to have a woman by his side who loved the life that he loved.

When he entered the cabin, she was in front of the fire, curled up on the couch with her knees drawn up to her chest, arms encircling them. Her back was to him, the side of her face lay against the sofa back. She appeared to be asleep, but he doubted that.

Chili with beans, grated cheese and crackers were on the stove, ready to eat. He could see from the den door there were no dirty dishes to show that she had eaten supper yet.

He went to her and placed a soft peck on top of her head. When she didn't respond, he turned back to kick off his boots beside the front door. He slid his jacket off of his shoulders and let it fall on top of the boots.

Jesse had hit the nail, so to speak, when he used the term, *silent treatment*. This had been going on for days and she had to be as sick of it as he was. He sat down beside her, keeping to his side of the small loveseat.

Oddly enough, she straightened herself and twisted around until she almost faced him, but kept her eyes on the flickering fire. He studied her face, her eyes from the side view. He saw fear there and to the degree that it made his heart sink another notch.

"You want to talk about what's bothering you, Reeny?"

After a few seconds, she nodded her head. "I don't know how to say it."

"Is it something from back before we met?"

She shook her head.

"Has somebody said something or done something that hurt your feelings? Did I?"

She didn't answer immediately. He knew he was close, but couldn't for the life of him, come up with anything he'd done to cause this.

She turned then and looked him in the eyes. "Why did you ask me to marry you?"

He glanced down and took himself back to that moment. When it hit him, he jerked his eyes back to meet hers. Where did she hear that from? It had to be *that.* It was the only reason he would have done such a thing, even though he soon fell madly in love with her. He may as well lay it out there and hope she could understand.

"I love you more than life, Reeny. You're my wife and I know we're meant to be together. But, I asked you to marry me back in Albuquerque because God told me to marry you."

"Did you really *want* to, or was it because you weren't given a choice?"

He sighed heavily. "Both."

"It can't be both."

"Yes, it can. I happen to believe love at first sight can happen. Maybe God causes it to happen, I don't know. But I felt drawn to you, Reeny, from the start. I mean, look at you—gorgeous blonde hair all over the place, beautiful face, cutest little behind I ever looked twice at. Now *you* look at *this."* He slapped a hand to his chest. "Do not even try to tell me, when you first saw *this,* you didn't instantly swoon and think *Greek god!*"

She rolled her eyes, a slight smile on her lips.

"Greek hop-a-long, maybe?"

She laughed then. Yes, she thought Greek god. And yes, she swooned. But she'd be hanged before he ever got that out of her. He'd never let it go.

A serious wrinkle creased her forehead. "How can you hear God say those kind of things…telling you to marry somebody?"

Hmm. How could he explain this? *Lord, can you help me out? How do I tell her how you talk to me?* In seconds, a scripture breezed through his mind.

"Well, the Bible says *My sheep hear My Voice.* So I know He wants us to hear Him speak to us. The first time I heard Him, I was around twelve—the day I buried my mom. I just always knew He talked to us, I guess. It's like I hear Him on the inside of me. His Spirit speaks into my spirit. Is that clear as mud?"

"No, I understand what you mean. I was just thinking that maybe God just told you to marry me to save me from those men. Then maybe you would…"

"Un-marry you?" He watched her swallow hard and look down at her knees. It was all he could do to keep from reaching for her to pull her into his arms. "Reeny, that's not how God works. He sent me to Albuquerque, led me to that park and led you to jump into my truck." He paused thoughtfully. "Now, because all that happened, doesn't mean we were supposed to stay together. I could have just been provided as a means of escape for you. But He *did* mean for us to stay together because He said so. You and I are called by God to be together. I know that as sure as I know my own name."

He cupped her chin and turned her face up to his. "Do you know this too? Can you feel it in your insides?"

Her eyes began to fill. "I know that I love you, Donny, so much that it makes me hurt bad to think of not being with you."

His hands slid to her upper arms and pulled her close into the curve of his body. With his mouth against the top of her head, he whispered shakily, "That's the first time you've ever said you loved me. You don't know how bad I've wanted to hear that from you."

The heaviness that had weighed her down ever since Granny Martha's revelation that Donny had been commanded by the Lord to marry her, finally lifted. She realized there were a lot of things she needed to learn about how and why she was led of God to be in this place and with this loving man and his family. In time, she would know. But for now, she was filled with hope and love and strangely, a desire to know God like her husband knows Him. She wanted to hear His Voice. It was as if something on the inside of her had awakened from a deep sleep. The intensity of the love welling from deep inside of her made her ache for her husband's arms, made her need for his joy to be full, for all of his desires to be met—Not just hers. There was something so real about her feelings with Donny—Something pure and good.

She sat up straight where she could see his face. A slow smile lifted the corners of his mouth—sexy, sweet and all for her. His lips brushed her forehead and she put her arms around his neck and clung to him. When their lips met this time, a passionate longing rocked her all the way to her toes. Pure physical sensations were grabbing her middle until her breaths were quick and shallow.

Donny responded with a tight wrap of his arms around her, but mindful still to allow her the option of slowing down or stopping. He deepened the kiss until he was afraid he might go too far and either not stop, or lose his mind. But he couldn't hold back. She wanted more from him this time. Something was different about her kisses. He knew if he scooped her up and carried her to bed, she would be all his for the first time.

Reeny was shocked at the inferno blazing inside of her. She had never felt anything like it, didn't know such a thing existed. And Donny was her husband. These feelings had to be a good thing—a sweet experience waiting to be completed.

Then somewhere in all the exquisite burning in her blood veins, she had a thought. Not a bad one, but one that seemed to pull her backward just a notch. It seemed to have come into her mind just for the purpose of cooling her down to give her a moment to consider it. Oh lord, could she stand to stop now? Could she do this to Donny after he had been so patient and waited on her all of this time, never taking liberties with her because of her past?

Yes! She could! She gently pulled herself out of his tight hold. She hated the pained look on his face knowing what she had just done to cause it. She was ready to make love with him. More than ready. But not here in this cabin. And for now, *she* was the only gift she could give to her husband. She would wait until her little surprise gathering of his family and friends for a quick, but real, wedding ceremony—A true wedding night surprise!

He wasn't sure where he got the willpower to turn her loose and then act like everything was okay. It wasn't. He closed his eyes for a moment and fought off the urge to be mad. At least this was progress, he consoled himself.

She reluctantly turned loose of him and stood up. "Are you hungry?"

He shook his head in disbelief. "Am I hungry, she asks? Are you trying to make me go nuts?"

"I'm sorry. Just give me a little more time." She tried to get out of that conversation. She didn't want or need more time, but she wanted him to have the most awesome wedding and wedding night with her and she would just have to pretend for a while. Hopefully she could put this surprise wedding together really soon. It would be a real ceremony to remember, hers and her sweet Donny's. And they could take a few pictures to show their children someday.

Before they headed to the kitchen for a chili and cracker feast, a knock sounded at the front door. Donny jumped up and swung it open.

"Hope we're not interrupting anything," Laura said.

"Don't matter if you are. Come in. What are you ladies up to tonight?"

Martha looked at her sidekick and could tell she wasn't going to be able to do this dirty little deed. So it was up to her to forge ahead. "Well, me and Laura was talking earlier, Reeny, about your wanting to have a little wedding get together for you and Donny to say your vows in front of all of us here, so we wanted to help and needed to see what date would be good for yall and get a plan down."

At the look on Reeny's face, Laura wanted to crawl back out the door and re-think this whole thing, but it was too late.

Martha's hide was tougher than Laura's and she proceeded on without batting a lash.

Donny looked surprised, glancing from Martha, then to Reeny.

Martha continued with the farce. "Is this not a good time for this?"

"I didn't know anything about this," Donny stated with hesitation. "Sounds nice though."

"Well, I…I meant for it to be a surprise for Donny. I guess I didn't make that clear when I mentioned it at Thanksgiving."

"Oh, Reeny, we're sorry," said Laura. "No, I guess we didn't get that part." She hoped her nose didn't shoot out a couple inches.

"Oh well, we can still plan a nice little ceremony." Martha tried to lighten the disappointment showing on Reeny, even though she and Laura both expected it. "How about us girls get together tomorrow then and get the details worked out. Hope you'll forgive us for spoiling the surprise. Dang our old hides, anyway!"

Reeny smiled as much as she could muster up. "There's nothing to forgive. We'll make plans tomorrow. It'll be fun." She refused to let that get her down. Not after all the wonderful things this family had done for her. She still had the night *of to* save as a surprise.

***

EPILOGUE

Three Weeks Later

It was Christmas Eve morning. Reeny was as excited as any little kid in a toy store. This was her first ever, real family Christmas. Trees were decorated and gifts wrapped. Garland and twinkle lights were strung here and there. Lots of food had already been prepared, including an oblong chocolate sheet cake with chocolate icing for the wedding ceremony that everybody agreed to include in all of their holiday doings. She made the cake herself along with Hank Walton's expert guidance. He said it was his input for the wedding.

They would all gather at two o'clock in Judd and Toni Luke's big log house living room. Since it already had holiday decorations up, that would take care of that part.

Les and Kaitlyn Kane offered to take pictures and, of course, Pastor Judd Luke would minister the, as Donny put it—last rites!

Reeny had insisted they stay in the guest cabin across the drive until after Christmas. She had revealed to Laura a couple of weeks ago, that she planned to move back into the Honeymoon Hideout on Christmas Eve after the ceremony. So, Laura made her promise to let her and Granny Martha tidy it up for them, as part of their wedding gift. She could hardly refuse a gift. The generosity of her new family and friends from this ranching community was overwhelming, to say the least.

And today was the day! Her and Donny's Christmas Eve wedding day. She fought off an attack of happy tears all morning.

At high noon, Laura, Granny Martha and Kaitlyn Kane showed up at the cabin and stole Reeny right out the front door. No explanation.

Immediately behind them came Jesse, Hank and Judd. They shoved their captive into Jesse's dually and headed for Hank's cabin.

"Hey, where are we going? My chocolate cake is the other way."

Nobody said a word.

"This is just *wrong!* That's what it is!"

They just laughed at him.

The women led Reeny across the drive to the ranch house. The two younger Brandon children were playing for the afternoon at the Luke's and Andy was helping out in Judd's barn.

After the group excitedly crowded into the master bedroom, they stood still and watched Reeny. She froze in surprise and awe. Hanging on the closet door was the most beautiful white wedding dress she'd ever seen in her life. Pearls streamed down the lace sleeves and around the midriff bodice. A string of white pearls hung on the coat hanger hook and were draped down the V-neck. The dress was full and floor length. A pair of white satin low heeled shoes was on the floor beside the dress. A long veil hung by a twisted pearl head band. She stood and stared at her wedding attire, fighting back tears of pure humbled joy. When she finally looked at the precious faces around her, she realized they had all lost the battle with their tears.

"I don't know what to say." She wouldn't dare tell them the thought that had just crossed her mind, but as much as she loved this, she was going to be a whole lot out of place dressed in this.

Martha seemed to have read her mind. "Now, you don't worry about being over-done for your wedding. This is really a day more for the bride anyway. Right, girls?"

"That's absolutely right," Kaitlyn assured her.

"Yes, guys aren't that wild about this day other than getting it over with," said Laura. "But they sure do like to see their little bride all dressed up."

They all knew that wasn't entirely the truth about their men or Donny either, but they needed to keep up her excitement.

"Yeah, we ruint your surprise for Donny, so we're making up for it. He'll really be surprised when you walk into that living room in this."

"And besides, you deserve this." Laura reached over and gave her a hug. "You've been putting up with that crack pot's practical jokes and sparing the rest of us around here. We're plumb grateful."

Reeny chuckled. "Well, now that you put it like that, maybe I do deserve it."

They all laughed and for the next hour they fussed with getting her long blonde tresses in a sweet feminine up-do and makeup put on to perfection.

The dress and shoes were last and fit her like they had been tailored for her body.

When it was time to go, Reeny was led over to a full length mirror to see herself for the first time. Her hair was piled on top of her head with the pearl head band circling the big loopy curls. Soft short tendrils framed her face and lay on the back of her neck. She had never worn makeup. The thin covering that had been applied to her cheeks, along with a pale pink lipstick and the barest touch of pink over her cheek bones made her think of a soft pastel butterfly just released from it's cocoon. Her eyes moved slowly down her front, to the pearl necklace that lay against her skin, to the satin and lace and pearls that hung in layers almost to the floor. The toes of her satin shoes completed the picture of the butterfly woman in the mirror. She was stunned at what she saw and knew her surprise hadn't been lost after all. This was far better than her original plan for her husband. *Thank You, Jesus, for my wonderful family and friends,* she offered silently.

"Reeny, you look like a storybook princess." Kaitlyn could hardly take her eyes from the image in the mirror where she stood at Reeny's shoulder. Their smiles met through the glass. The two women shared a common loss of their infant babies and had become closer friends after Reeny's ordeal. Reeny was amazed at how God seemed to meet the needs of His people. He was there at every bend in the road. He certainly had been for her.

"Girls, it's time to get this show on the road." Martha gathered up the longest and fullest part of Reeny's dress in the back and held it up while they got her coat on her and loaded up in Laura's SUV.

When they were finally underway to the Double OO, Kaitlyn let Reeny in on the last part of her attire that she hadn't seen yet. "Sorry to do this to you, but here, put this on." She handed her a black mask to cover her eyes.

"You're kidding me. Say you're kidding."

"Nope. Came with the dress. You have to wear it," Martha quipped, drawing laughter.

"Now yall are scaring me," she laughed and let Kaitlyn secure the mask over her eyes. "Are we still going to the Luke's for the ceremony?"

"Yes, we are. We're arriving now and it looks like one of our members from Cowboy Church showed up. As she drove past the lineup of vehicles that trailed all the way down the long drive, she knew the charade was a success. She grinned and drove past the house and down the hill to the Double OO barn and indoor arena.

Everybody was quiet while they escorted her inside to the designated *Reeny spot* in the ally of the barn. The horses didn't get the message and were as noisy as they could possibly get.

"Is that hor…?" Reeny's senses were on high alert.

"Shhh!" Martha bumped her on the arm. "This is a surprise, remember?"

Laura and Kaitlyn had to stifle giggles. They couldn't believe how this was going until they looked up to see Jesse, Hank and Judd walk inside the barn from the opposite end guiding the blindfolded groom. The three women standing with Reeny almost lost it when they saw the gag in Donny's mouth.

Flashes were going off from every angle as Toni Luke moved around silently and carefully aiming her camera. It took her a minute to compose herself when she saw the gagged groom.

The couple, along with their separate entourages, stood on either side of the entrance to the indoor arena. Neither the bride nor groom was aware of the other one's presence.

The women couldn't say a word, but took in Donny from head to toe. His white tux, complete with all white accessories was a sight to behold. Laura fanned her own face with her hand trying to hold off the gathering tears. Who was going to be the most surprised? It wasn't hard to guess that one.

Pastor Judd left to take his place.

Finally, with Donny and Reeny unknowingly facing each other only six feet apart, the gag was removed first, and then both blindfolds were removed at the same time by Laura and Jesse. All others had gone inside the arena to take their seat.

It took a few seconds for their eyes to adjust and realize what and who they were looking at.

Donny's eyes grew, along with his speechless mouth. He couldn't move or suck a decent breath. Not in his lifetime had he ever seen such a beautiful thing as this woman, this angel, *his wife,* who stood in front of him, staring with her mouth wide open.

Reeny was in shock. She couldn't find a word one anywhere inside of her head. She couldn't move her eyes from the face of her husband, her cowboy, her crack pot, funny man who was looking at her with eyes of pure adoration and standing there dressed like a prince. And he was hers.

Music suddenly sounded from somewhere inside of the arena. When their heads turned toward the intro to the Wedding March, Jesse and Laura, still standing behind them, pushed them together and turned them to face the arena entrance.

A four foot width of deep red carpet stretched in front of them to form a center aisle. People were standing on both sides of the red walkway and all of them turned to face the bride and groom. Laura held out a beautiful arrangement of wild flowers with mixed greenery and white ribbon—the bride's bouquet.

But neither the bride nor the groom saw any of it, nor seemed aware of the bouquet silently placed into Reeny's hands. All watched their faces as a mesmerized awe fell in a hush on both of them. They didn't seem to be fully aware of each other now. At the far end of the red carpet, stood their focus—a ten foot high Aspen log Cross stood as a wedding alter—tall and glorious, draped in Christmas garland and twinkle lights. Red ribbon was twisted into the silver garland that graced the entire Cross. Pots of poinsettias encircled the area around its base to form a spot for the bride and groom to stand.

As the music continued to play, Donny reached for his wife's hand, not moving his eyes from the top of the Cross, and together they walked, slowly, awed by the beauty of the sacred symbol in front of them. As they reached their place at the foot, they simultaneously dropped onto their knees. Donny pulled his wife into his arms and they held to each other as Pastor Judd kneeled, tears streaming, in front of them and they repeated their vows to each other.

Donny held the face of his bride as he softly kissed her and when they stood up and turned to face their guests, there wasn't a dry eye in the barn, including the bride and groom. For once, Donny didn't have a joke in him.

Jesse and Laura were the first to gather the couple in hugs and Hank and Martha joined them, still swiping at trickling tears. Most of their friends and acquaintances from Cowboy

Church were there to witness this holy moment. Everyone was aware of what Donny and Reeny had been through.

Finally, all made their way up the hill to the house where a reception had been prepared, complete with the groom's own chocolate cake as well as a three tier white wedding cake decorated with all the bells and whistles.

An hour or so later, with the guests all filing out at once, Laura and Jesse urged the newlyweds to go on home. In fact, they practically pushed the still amazed couple toward the front door.

"We'll clean up here and head home in a while. We've got Santa to get ready for." Laura hurried them up.

"Ranch truck is out front. Go on. See you two tomorrow. Merry Christmas." Jesse opened the front door.

As soon as they stepped outside, mounds of bird seed popped them from all sides, all the way to the old dually. The door to the back seat was open. Hank revved and gunned the burned out mufflers for special effects from the *secret* get-away vehicle and waved his arm out the window. Martha was standing up in the doorframe on the step plate of the truck on her passenger side and letting loose with her arsenal of seeds from over the top of the cab.

Five minutes later, Hank roared through the High Point ranch gate, past the house and then the barn. He dropped his passengers in front of the Honeymoon Hideout. He and Martha both got out too and hand in hand, strolled back toward the ranch yard. "Merry Christmas," they called back nearly in unison.

Donny stood beside his bride. He looked at the cabin and then, back to her. "Did you know about this?"

She smiled, her eyes twinkling a message into his that he understood.

He ran up the steps and swung the door open, then raced back down, slightly tripping in his haste. Reeny burst out laughing as he swung her up into his arms and hauled her across the threshold into a cabin that left them both spell bound in the doorway.

A twinkling Christmas tree covered the little table beside the fireplace where a tiny flame licked at the logs. Green garland wrapped in red and silver ribbon and bows and more little twinkle lights encircled the wall of the entire bedroom/den. A sweet holiday aroma scented the air.

He stood her on her feet and pushed the door shut behind them. His arms went around her, but kept his distance just enough to look down into her shining face. "I need us to be really clear about this. That look you just flashed at me—Did it mean what I think it means?"

Her smile was slow and sweet. "I want to be your wife, Donny Brandon, all the way. I've been ready for this for a while now, but I wanted to wait until tonight. I meant to make this wedding and..." she gestured at the cozy, intimate setting of the cabin, "our little honeymoon in the hideout here, a special surprise for *you.* But it appears we both got the surprise of our lives. Your family is so awesome."

"*Our* family, Mrs. Donny Brandon."

He squinted at the pearl band that held her veil on and then reached both hands up to gently work it loose and lift it off of her head. The pins holding her hair up were next to go. He dropped it all on the floor as he kissed her, slow and gentle. His fingers threaded through her long heavy curls that now hung down her back.

"Did you just mess up my fancy hair do?" she whispered against his mouth.

"Nope, not yet. You haven't *seen* messed up hair."

She grasped either side of his face, pulled his head down and planted a quick, hard kiss on his lips. "Well, show me some, cowboy."

It took a few seconds for her words to sink in before he groaned like he was in the throes of a fit, then twisted around and clicked the lock on the cabin door.

****

PREVIEW OF

BOOK FIVE IN THE

SURRENDERED SERIES

SURRENDERED V PREVIEW

Carly felt almost drugged with sleep, like she'd been asleep for hours. But something was pulling her back to the surface of consciousness. Finally, she woke up and sat up trying to recognize through the dark, where she was. It was eerily quiet for the first few seconds, then the howling and yelping of a whole bunch of something froze her body, except for her heart rate that was pounding nine-0.

She was in a teepee stuck off by herself! "Oh no," she choked out behind her hands that now covered her face. Was it wolves? The squealing was endless and sounded as if they'd surrounded her.

Finally the noise faded away, but Carly was petrified. She was alone in a wilderness of wild animals and God only knew what else.

She got up and rushed over to turn on the lamp. Pop! The bulb blew. The darkness was trying to choke her now. She got to the door and remembered seeing two long, white terry robes hanging on the hook on the inside of the door. She grabbed one and put it on as she unlocked the bolt and peeped outside. Not much moonlight—it was too quiet now.

She fixed her eyes on the spot that Beau had pointed out to her—where his cabin set. Keeping her sight on that general area, she ran toward it. Fear had an ugly grip on her, she could barely breathe. Her heart hammered. She'd always been afraid of the dark. She'd been scared silly by three big brothers who would hide in a darkened room and jump out at her, screeching like ghouls. It seemed to be their favorite past time, but they'd left her scarred for life. She'd never fully recovered from a fear of darkness.

There it was. She saw a porch light of Beau's cabin and raced for the door knob. It was locked.

"Beau!" She knocked with her knuckles, then pounded with her fists. "Beau!"

She spied a single window and hoped that was his bedroom. She stepped just off the small porch and pounded on the glass panes hard and loud enough to wake the dead.

"Beau!"

"What in the...!" Beau raised up and rubbed his face before hitting the floor at a run as his brain began to register. He had no idea who or what, but he'd heard his name.

Just then the screaming yelps came again right behind her. She jumped back onto the porch and threw herself against the door at the same moment Beau jerked it open. Her momentum was such that the force surprised him and both of them landed in a painful heap on the floor between the loveseat and the fireplace.

Beau lay still, working hard to get his breath. He was fully aware that someone—a female someone—was spread out on top of him, her arms around his neck like a tightened hanging noose. He knew she was a she because he could hear her female voice crying hysterically.

Finally he grabbed her arms and pulled, freeing his airway and vocal chords. She jerked her arms loose and got a second hold on him.

This time he gripped her arms and pulled hard. "Hey...stop it! Stop it!" A slight shake on her arms got her attention.

When she jerked her face up from the middle of his chest, Beau saw it was Carly Jones, stark terror almost making her recognizable.

"W...wolves! A pack of wolves!"

He glanced toward the open door and listened. All he could hear was her quick breaths and a whimper here and there.

"Take a deep breath, Carly. You're okay. I'm sure they're gone now."

Realizing for the first time that Beau was beneath her on the floor, she slid off to the side of him and sat up, pulling the terry robe back tight around her. She could feel the roots of her hair burning. "I'm...so sorry." She sniffled and swiped at her wet cheeks.

"There's no harm done." *Except for a couple of dislocated shoulder blades.* He stood up, and then helped her to her feet. "You okay now?"

She nodded her head and turned to look out the door.

Beau shut the door and flipped on a lamp. "You want to tell me what happened?"

“I woke up and heard loud screaming and yelping like a pack of dogs. They sounded like they were about to tear through my teepee. I heard them more than once and I turned on the lamp, but the bulb went out and it was dark. It...it was dark.”

He heard every word she was saying. She thought wolves were after her and she’s scared of the dark. At the same time, he was seeing a beautiful mess of tangled blond hair, deep sea green eyes that were wet with tears of fright and a young woman who needed someone to help her feel safe.

“Coyotes.” He spoke low and calmly. “They run in packs like that and sometimes sound closer than they actually are. You’re not in any danger, Carly.

Just then, he heard their yelping again and reopened the door. “Step out here.” He grasped her arm when she started to back away and pulled her with him. He pressed an arm around her shoulders and stood with her on the porch while he let her listen to a chorus of the wild animal sounds he loved the most, but in the safety of his embrace. He watched her face and saw the fear leave—replaced with a big-eyed awe. He smiled down at her and she leaned closer into his side.

www.ingramcontent.com/pod-product-compliance
Lightning Source LLC
Chambersburg PA
CBHW031308120626
46554CB00001BA/333

* 9 7 8 0 9 9 6 2 9 5 9 3 2 *